Rachel Landon, Feeling Abandoned

Rachel Landon

Feeling Abandoned

A Journey Toward Forgiveness

by Allie Slocum

Copyright © 2019 by Allie Slocum

This book is a work of fiction. Names, characters, and incidents are either the product of the author's imagination or are based on personal experiences with friends and have been used with permission.

Appeals to third through sixth graders.

Cover design by Todd Slocum, artwork by Kaylie Slocum, title by Rylie Slocum

ISBN: 9781081914714

www.characterclubonline.com

This book is dedicated to the girls of the second generation of Character Club–some of whom participated in my home for three years:

Bella, Eva, Journey, Lily W., Lilly S., Olivia, and Rylie

Remember that you are special and always...

Speak Life!

Preface

Teachers, you may access the discussion questions included at the end of this book to help students respond in journals or in group discussions. For actual project ideas, visit

www.characterclubonline.com

These stories were birthed from the desire to instill strong character virtues in children. Allie started Character Club with thirteen girls when her oldest daughter was in third grade. It grew to eighteen students by the time her daughter was in fifth grade. Allie then started a coed club at her church. Now she is teaching the second generation of Character Club with her younger daughter's age group. She is forever looking for good stories that students can relate to with applicable lessons and activities. She hopes these books and website will inspire students *and* teachers.

Acknowledgments

I am always so grateful to the many people who show up to be a part of the team to make a book possible. This one is no exception.

Always first, my Creator, author of all creativity. Thank you for the continued flow of ideas for each story.

Todd Slocum, the most creative & patient, husband & human I know. Thank you for all the time you spend helping make these books come to fruition. Kaylie and Rylie, my two favorite young people and daughters, who amaze me with their creativity each day. Thank you for the artwork and title.

Deb Hall, editor extraordinaire and friend–thanks for your patience answering my endless last minute questions.

My first Beta readers: Alicia, Sandy, Sharon–thanks for your enthusiasm for the series.

7th grade focus group: Aspen, Ellie, Jordyn, Kaitlynn, and Kaylie–thanks for helping me decide how to make this story better.

Students in the elementary focus group: Ashlyn, Braelyn, Carson, Declan, Holden, Isabella, Jackie, Jacob, Journey, Kelly, Kieran, Owen, Lilly, Loralei, Maisie, Miles P., Miles U., Patty, Rene, and Rylie–your ideas were both helpful and hilarious.

Christy Jeppesen, superfan and co-worker–thanks for your input, enthusiasm, and support for this series. Sue Greeley–you surprise me every time you look at something. Abby, Ruth and Carrie – your last minute insights are helpful every time! Thank you.

Message to the Reader:

In case you experience déjà vu during the first chapter, I'd like to let you in on a little secret. The scene that unfolds at Character Club also appeared in *Jeanie Blair, Author Extraordinaire*. In this book, you are seeing that same incident through Rachel's eyes. So sit back, relax, and enjoy the story. In fact, all the Character Club Series books overlap to some degree as they take place in a single school year. As you read the various books, you will find secret nuggets that connect each with one another. Sometimes these overlap points will be obvious. Sometimes they will be subtle. I hope you enjoy the Character Club series!

~Allie Slocum

Mrs. Keller's Calendar of Virtues:

Fall Semester
September - Compassion
October - Forgiveness
November - Integrity
December - Respect

Spring Semester
January - Responsibility
February - Initiative
March - Cooperation
April - Perseverance

Character Club Cast of Characters*

Mrs. Keller - teacher
Andrew Keller - high school son
Karlie Keller - high school daughter

Girls:
Jeanie & Claire - best friends
Angel - soccer star
Amanda, Maria & Valerie - inseparable threesome
Rachel & Maggie - best friends
Tanya & Tia - sisters
Wendy - military family member

Boys:
Ethan - soccer star
John & Jack - twins
Lucas - older, quiet supporter
Peter & Cayden - worm throwers
Theo & Noah - good friends

Not all characters are named in every book.

Contents

1 ~ Math Madness

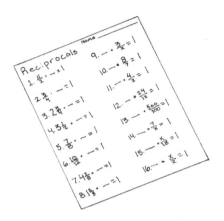

Alone.

That's how twelve-year-old Rachel Landon always seemed to feel. She felt it now as she scrambled down the hall to get to her next class. She'd become absorbed in a daydream of misery after reading a text from her dad. He was going to be working late again tonight. That meant another frozen dinner and nothing but the television to keep her company. The class bell snapped Rachel out of her reverie. She was late.

As Rachel rounded the corner, still glancing at her phone, she slid on a jacket left on the floor. Rachel lost her balance and crashed to the floor in a painful split. She was no gymnast. Books flew all over the hall. Rachel looked behind her to see if anyone had witnessed the wipeout. The corridor was empty. Rachel checked her phone to make sure she hadn't cracked the glass . . . again. It survived this time.

As she collected her books and stood, she saw Jeanie Blair down the hall. Jeanie must have walked out of a classroom after Rachel fell. Jeanie made eye contact with Rachel for a second, then she disappeared into a nearby room.

Rachel didn't know Jeanie very well, but they both went to Character Club. Character Club met every Thursday after school at Mrs. Keller's house. Mrs. Keller was a schoolteacher before she had children. When her kids were born, she decided to start a club for kids to teach them different character values. Now, her own kids were in high school, and during Character Club meetings they helped out with snacks, games, and crowd control.

"It would've been nice if she had checked on me rather than disappearing," Rachel thought as she brushed off the back pockets of her white jeans. She headed to math class walking like someone who'd ridden a horse all day for the first time.

Rachel's math teacher, Mr. Bittel, gave her the "we'll talk later" look as she slunk into class. She was only a minute late, but he didn't have much grace. Confirming her assessment of his look, he said, "Come see me after class, Miss Landon."

Rachel collapsed into her seat. She glanced at her neighbor's desk to catch the page number and opened her book.

Her thoughts drifted back to her dad's text. At least it was Thursday and she would have Character Club for a few hours after school. Maggie had tried to drag Rachel there all last year. Maggie was Rachel's best friend. Maggie was short for Margaret, the name that had been given to every first female in her family for generations. If you called her Margaret, though, be prepared to get a whack upside the head.

The girls had met before kindergarten when they were in preschool. Their parents had both visited Miller Academy on the same day. Their moms exchanged phone numbers. Maggie and Rachel had playdates once a week all summer long. Rachel couldn't really remember life before Maggie. Maggie's mom was very memorable as well. She dressed like a hippie and always put flowers in Maggie's curly dark hair. Maggie still showed up with a flower in her hair some days. Maggie was bigger-boned than Rachel, but she played soccer and kept in shape.

Rachel finally joined Maggie at Character Club a few weeks ago when school started back up. It seemed like a great way to get to know different kids from school. She needed some change.

Maggie hadn't succeeded in dragging their whole group to Character Club. Rachel, Maggie, Dani, and Laura had been a tribe since first grade when their teacher, Mrs. Dish, put them into a group for a log cabin project. The four of them built the most amazing copy of a pioneer cabin the class had ever seen. Dani's dad was an architect in town. Just about every new house was built by his company. He spearheaded any building project the girls ever worked on. Dani's mom bought them anything they wanted to "dress things up a bit."

But things had changed since Rachel's mom's accident. Dani and Laura seemed a bit more distant. Dani didn't invite Rachel over anymore. Thankfully, Maggie had Rachel over twice as much to make up for it. It was easy to forget about problems at Maggie's house. She had three younger siblings: Marley, Maddox, and Megan. They were always chasing Rachel with a toy airplane, rainbow wand, or unicorn. Maggie's mom always had a diffuser with some kind of calming oil, pumping wonderful smells into the air.

Today, as Mr. Bittel explained improper fractions, Rachel scanned the room with her eyes. Maggie and Laura weren't in Rachel's math class. Dani was and sat beside her. Her shiny black hair changed styles monthly. Right now, it was cut in a crisp, clean A-line style. Dani was four inches taller than Rachel. Her dark eyes could penetrate walls. With her fancy clothes, she looked like a model most of the time. Today she wore five bangle bracelets on her arm. Rachel wore her old yellow T-shirt and favorite white jeans. She knew it was past season to wear white, but these fit her like an old friend. The only thing that matched on the two of them were the crisscrossed bobby pins this morning's text had told them all to wear in their hair.

Math came easy to Rachel. She found herself always counting things. She knew there were eight framed pictures, six math posters, and three clocks in the room. Her mom always used to brag about how proud she was of Rachel's mathematical mind. Rachel wished her dad took notice of this—or anything about her, for that matter. Since her mom's accident, he had poured his life into his job and never seemed to notice anything else.

So when Brian Matthews seemed to start noticing her, Rachel paid attention. Brian sat one aisle over and one seat in front of her, on the opposite side of Dani. Rachel enjoyed staring at his profile during Mr. Bittel's math lectures. Brian's strong cheekbones and blond hair made him look like some sort of superhero.

Mr. Bittel called on Brian to give the improper fraction for two and three-fourths. Silence filled the room until Brian admitted, "I just don't get it, Mr. Bittel."

"Maybe if you paid better attention, it wouldn't be so difficult," Mr. Bittel chided.

Rachel really didn't think Brian wasn't paying attention. She raised her hand. "Yes, Miss Landon."

"If you multiply the two times the four, then add three, you get eleven-fourths."

"Correct. Now, who can tell me the opposite of eleven-fourths?"

"Negative eleven-fourths," Lucas offered. Lucas went to Character Club too. He always treated everyone with respect. He looked like a hero too, with his dark hair, green eyes, and dimpled smile.

"Yes. The opposite of a positive number is always the negative and vice versa. Who can give me the absolute value of negative two and three- fourths?"

Dani sat straight up in her perfectly

pressed blouse and raised her hand. Dani never volunteered in class, so Rachel knew she was up to something. When Mr. Bittel looked her way, Dani said, "Mr. Bittel, all this talk about negatives is giving me negative thoughts."

Several boys laughed out loud. Rachel groaned. Mr. Bittel just looked at Dani over his glasses and said to the class, "Now remember, positive or negative, numbers with equal distances from zero have the same absolute value. What is the absolute value of our number?"

No one volunteered. Finally Mr. Bittel drafted Rachel to share the answer.

"It's two and three-fourths," she answered shyly.

"Correct. Thank you, Rachel." He turned to the class. "You can all partner up and begin working on the assignment. If anyone needs personal instruction, I'll be here at my desk."

Brian immediately turned toward Rachel and asked to partner with her. Rachel nodded with surprise. Rachel usually worked with Dani, but this called for an exception. The two of them scooted their desks together while other classmates rearranged themselves. Rachel missed the perturbed look on Dani's face when she lost her partner to Brian. Dani turned her model figure away and snatched Lucas for a partner.

Brian leaned over Rachel's desk, and they got to work. Rachel hoped Brian couldn't hear her heart pounding out of her chest.

"You make it seem so easy," Brian confided in her.

"Math is just one of those things that clicks for me." She smiled at him.

"Thank goodness for that," he quipped. Rachel guided Brian through each problem step by step. They finished the last problem with time to spare. Brian started to grab his graphic novel as Rachel opened her sketchbook. Brian stopped to watch Rachel as she started sketching Mr. Bittel. Rachel showed him how she starts with the eyes. Mr. Bittel's were small, dark, and beady. She sketched his glasses around them. Then she added his pointy nose and tight mustache. She was forming the shape of his bald head around his features when the bell rang.

"You're really good," Brian said before he headed out the door to lunch. "Maybe you can draw me next time."

Rachel smiled and collected her things.

Mr. Bittel waited at his desk for her to stop by. He peered over his glasses at her. "And why were you tardy, Miss Landon?"

"I slipped and fell in the hallway. My books and papers scattered all over. It took me some time to gather it all up. I'm very sorry."

Mr. Bittel pursed his lips and considered her a moment. "Very well. This is only your first offense. I'll let it slide this time. Don't let it happen again."

"I won't, Mr. Bittel." Rachel turned and scooted out the door before he changed his mind.

When Rachel arrived at the regular lunchroom table, Dani was waiting with a fierce look on her face. She pointed a perfectly manicured fingernail in front of Rachel's face and snarled, "Stay away from Brian Matthews, Rachel."

Dani stood up with her tray and stomped

away in her brand-new designer sandals. Laura looked up at Rachel and shrugged.

Rachel, thoroughly confused, watched her leave. Maggie came up behind her and said, "Somebody didn't get enough sleep last night. What's with Dani?"

Rachel shrugged. "Hope she's happier tomorrow."

After school, Maggie and Rachel found Angel and Wendy, two other girls who went to Character Club. Angel tightened her long black ponytail like she was getting ready for a race. She could outrun most of the boys. Wendy pushed her bright pink glasses up on her nose and tucked some of her dark blonde hair behind her ear. The four walked to Mrs. Keller's house together. Angel led the way while the other three tried to keep up.

Most of the kids walked in groups, as Mrs. Keller lived only two blocks from school. Rachel was huffing by the time they rounded the last corner. A flock of geese flew over their heads.

"Wow," Maggie said. "How many?"

"Twenty-one," Rachel said without

thinking.

Maggie chuckled. She was always quizzing Rachel on how many cars, birds, trees there were, whatever it was. Rachel never even thought about it.

When they arrived, Wendy went to sit with Mrs. Keller. She had brought something special to show the group, but she'd kept it a secret from them. Angel joined the soccer game already in progress in the backyard. Maggie stopped in the kitchen to load up on some snacks before she ventured outside to join the soccer game.

Rachel usually played too, but today she felt like she needed to sketch. Sketching always calmed her down when she was upset or stressed, which lately felt like all the time. After grabbing her own snack from the kitchen, she wandered outside to the back patio. Mrs. Keller had two red couches in the corner near her beautiful garden.

Rachel crossed the patio and made herself comfortable on the farthest couch. Her back was to the garden where Peter and Cayden, two troublemakers, were studying something in the dirt. They didn't even seem to notice her. She watched a girl she didn't know pass the soccer ball to Angel. Angel attempted to score against Ethan McWyer on the other team. Angel and Ethan were the best at the sport and very competitive with each other. Ethan was just about the only boy Angel couldn't beat in a race.

Lucas blocked her shot and passed it back to Ethan. The twin boys were also playing, but Rachel couldn't remember their names. Angel charged after the ball in attack mode.

Rachel pulled out her sketchbook thinking that she could sketch the soccer game. Her mind wandered as she let her thoughts lead her pencil. She realized she was sketching Brian's face instead.

Rachel heard the sliding glass door open. She looked up to see Jeanie walk out the door, grab a water bottle, and head to the back corner of the yard. Jeanie walked under the arbor and sat down in Mrs. Keller's solo Adirondack chair. She was almost completely hidden from sight. Rachel watched her pull out a notebook. Jeanie usually played soccer

13

too. Maybe Jeanie was feeling the same way as Rachel today, needing to be alone. Maybe that's why she didn't seem very compassionate when Rachel slipped at school.

Rachel began comparing herself with Jeanie. Maybe they were a lot alike. Same brown hair. Same . . . Rachel couldn't think of anything else. Maybe they weren't that similar.

Rachel continued to sketch. Then she turned her attention to two girls she had been told were sisters. One was pushing the other on the swing hanging from Mrs. Keller's cottonwood tree. Rachel watched them switch places. They looked so happy and carefree. Rachel wondered what their family was like. She returned to her sketch, now taking shape. She closed her eyes for a moment to remember more detail in Brian's face.

Suddenly, she felt something plop on her lap, followed by loud laughter. She opened her eyes to find two wiggly, squiggly worms in her lap. Rachel shrieked. She jumped up, throwing her sketchbook into the air and flinging the worms onto the patio.

Rachel brushed off her jeans in disgust,

making sure there weren't any worm parts hanging on. As she did, she noticed her once-white jeans were now stained. She hardly heard all the commotion from the soccer ball being shot around the backyard like a pinball between kids—from Angel's swift sideways kick to Ethan's deflecting arm to the feet of the girl swinging to Cayden's unprotected side, causing Cayden to collapse. Peter fell backward belly-laughing as he ducked down behind the couch. Rachel looked up to see Mrs. Keller's teenage son, Andrew, come running out of the house.

Andrew was more handsome than Brian and Lucas put together. His dark hair and dark, kind eyes made him seem mysterious in a way. All the girls adored him, but he was more the protective big-brother type to Rachel. Now he played a real hero as he took her arm and asked if she was okay. Stunned, Rachel nodded. Andrew pulled the boys aside to have an intense talk with them.

Maggie came running over from the soccer game to check on Rachel. "Oh my gosh!" she exclaimed. "Your favorite jeans!"

Rachel blinked back tears when she realized how good a friend Maggie was to know this fact. Maggie saw the tears coming and redirected. "Oh no. We're not breaking that dam today. Let's get you inside and clean those right up."

They headed inside toward the bathroom. Maggie grabbed some tissues from the end table as they passed through the family room. Wendy looked alarmed when she saw Rachel's face. Mrs. Keller was already headed outside to round everyone up to begin her lesson.

"Yoo-hoo!" Mrs. Keller called in her special way. "It's time to begin. Please show responsibility and clean up your snacks, then join me in our family room."

Rachel dabbed her eyes and said, "I'm okay. Let's just sit down."

"Are you sure?" The look in Maggie's eyes was full of concern.

"Yeah."

The two girls sat down on the carpet in Mrs. Keller's cozy family room as everyone else filed in. Andrew came in last, right behind

Peter and Cayden. He had convinced the boys to give an apology.

It felt pretty weak to Rachel. Apparently Mrs. Keller thought it was, too, because she asked them to try again.

"Wouldn't it be more heartfelt to look the person in the eye?" Mrs. Keller said as she looked right at Peter. "And if we actually mean to make amends, we also ask for forgiveness."

Rachel felt the pink creeping into her cheeks. She sniffed and kept her eyes glued to the spot on her jeans she couldn't stop rubbing.

Using Andrew as a safety buffer between themselves and Rachel, they each glanced at her quickly and said in unison, "I'm sorry, Rachel. Will you forgive me?"

Rachel glanced up, met their gaze, and nodded her head all within a split second. She didn't really forgive them, but she wanted to get all this attention off her. She really only wanted the attention of two people: Brian and her dad. A whole room full of girls and boys she hardly knew? No thanks. She wished she could disappear. Maggie slipped her arm around Rachel's shoulder.

Thankfully, Mrs. Keller was satisfied. She invited Wendy up to share her great-grandfather's life story and how he had earned a Purple Heart, which was Wendy's mysterious item. Rachel struggled to listen as the smudge on her jeans preoccupied her thoughts.

Nevertheless, Karlie, Mrs. Keller's daughter, caught Rachel's attention with the captivating story of the life of Clara Barton. Rachel had heard stories about how Karlie dressed in character sometimes. It really made the stories come to life. Karlie talked about compassion. Rachel softened her heart a little toward the boys, but she couldn't stop perseverating on the worm incident.

When club ended, kids straggled toward their homes. Some walked. Some had parents pick them up. Rachel liked to wait to walk home until after Maggie left. Sometimes Maggie's mom gave Rachel a ride even though she only lived about a ten-minute walk away.

After most of the kids left, the remaining students chatted inside or played soccer outside with Andrew until their parents arrived. Maggie tried to get Rachel back into the bathroom to clean up her jeans, but Rachel refused the help. She would wash and scrub them when she got home and hope for the best.

The soccer game broke up and the outside crowd came in. Ethan strolled in from the backyard holding up Rachel's sketchbook. "I found this on the patio. Anyone want to claim it?"

"Oooh, is that Brian Matthews?" Maria teased as she looked at the sketch. Valerie, Amanda, and Maria were three girls who always hung out together. They were huddled on the floor looking at one of Mrs. Keller's old scrapbooks. At Maria's comment, the other two looked up.

Amanda, a redhead with four older sisters and a flair for the dramatic, answered with a giggle, "Oh my gosh! Yes! Who's in love with Brian Matthews?"

Valerie pointed to the picture and covered her mouth with her other hand.

Rachel dropped her head to the floor as she thought, "Could this day get any worse?"

Then Peter said, "That's Rachel's."

And she knew the answer was yes.

2 ~ The Twisted Tale

Rachel scrambled to collect her things as the giggles swarmed around her. She needed to get away from this embarrassment. Karlie called from the front room that Maggie's mom had arrived. Maggie grabbed Rachel's arm and said, "Let's ask my mom if you can come home with me tonight." Lately Rachel really felt like a member of the Walters family. She spent almost as much time there as she did at home. With four kids, one extra didn't seem to matter. Rachel figured Maggie's mom missed her mom just as much as she did. Maybe it helped having Rachel around.

The girls walked out the front door. They found Mrs. Keller chatting through the front window of Mrs. Walters's old brown VW van.

Maggie's three-year-old sister, Megan, sat strapped in the backseat with the sliding door open. She bounced her short legs on the seat and waved her stuffed unicorn at the girls. Maggie's two brothers were nowhere in sight. Maggie's mom nodded to the girls. Rachel waved with the greeting, "Hi, Mrs. Walters. Hi, Meggie Moo-oo."

Megan glanced at Rachel when she heard Rachel's special call for her. She mooed back at her, then turned right back toward Mrs. Keller. Rachel could tell Megan was thinking hard about something. She usually asked questions faster than you could answer them.

Maggie opened her mouth to ask if Rachel could come home with them, but Megan blurted out, "Mommy, why does dat lady have such big butt?"

Mrs. Walters's face turned beet red as

she shushed Megan and motioned Maggie toward the car. "Let's go!"

Mrs. Keller just laughed with a wave of her hand. "Thank goodness I don't see my backside all that often. There's a reason God didn't give us eyes in the back of our heads!"

"Mommy!" Megan roared. "You said you DID hab eyes in da back your head! You lied!"

Maggie sheepishly climbed through the open door. Poor Mrs. Walters's face turned an even deeper shade of purple as she squealed her van away from the curb. Maggie didn't even have·time to shut the door, let alone ask if Rachel could join them.

Mrs. Keller and Rachel stood alone on the sidewalk as the van tore down the street. Rachel pondered Mrs. Keller's comment. If some kid had called her butt big, she would have been mortified.

Mrs. Keller seemed to read her mind and said, "Out of the mouth of babes . . . well, you never know what you might get! She didn't mean any harm, though. How are you holding up?"

"I'll be okay." Rachel shrugged.

Mrs. Keller gave Rachel a reassuring hug. "Just tell your mom to use extra stain stick. I think those worm smudges will come right out."

"Okay. Thanks. See you next week." Rachel gave a little wave and began her walk home. She didn't have the energy to clarify to Mrs. Keller that she would be doing her own laundry. She didn't have the heart to explain that her mom wasn't in the picture. She wished she could have gone home with Maggie.

As Rachel inhaled the floral scents along the walk home, her mood restored a little. It was close to a mile walk, but she passed beautiful homes and flower gardens on both sides of the street.

Today she followed her favorite route. It passed by two of her dream houses. The first house boasted tall purple flowers mixed with yellow bushes and pink roses. Rachel checked the swing attached to a tall tree behind the fence in the backyard. Sometimes there were little children playing on it.

Rachel wished she wasn't an only child,

especially since her mother was gone and her dad worked so much. But she realized that would just mean another mouth to feed. They were barely scraping by as it was, despite how many extra hours her dad put in.

The second house hardly had any front lawn at all. A giant porch wrapped all the way around it. Tall white columns held the porch in place. All along the edge where the sun could warm them sat different-sized pots overflowing with colorful flowers. Pots also rested on different thicknesses and heights of old tree trunks. The mathematician in Rachel counted them once. Sixty-eight pots! Every single one contained unique combinations of flowers and colors. Rachel slowed to almost a crawl every time she passed this house. She longed to settle herself on the front lawn and sketch that porch.

When she arrived at her empty house, Rachel dropped her backpack inside the door. She headed upstairs to her room. Rachel pulled off her once-white jeans and yellow T-shirt, threw on some gray sweatpants and a baggy yellow sweatshirt, and slipped into bed. She didn't have the energy to tackle the wash right this minute. Rachel never wore her clothes in her bed, even when they didn't have worm stains on them.

Rachel woke up an hour later with a start. She dreamed that Peter and Cayden had thrown a python on her and it tried to squeeze the life out of her. She rolled out of bed, and picking up her jeans, she headed to the laundry room. She rubbed the stain with an off-brand stain stick. Then she sprayed them with some generic liquid detergent and let them sit awhile before throwing them in the wash.

Rachel wandered out to the kitchen and washed her hands. She opened the freezer. There were tons of TV dinners to choose from, so she grabbed a fiesta chicken and put it in the microwave. Her phone buzzed. Her dad had bought her a cheap cell phone last year after the accident. He said it was for safety since he worked such crazy hours.

Dani had been so jealous because Rachel was the first in her class to have a smartphone. But Dani boasted about hers the very next week. They traded passcodes so there would never be any secrets between them—ever! Rachel would have traded the phone to have her dad home right now. Most of Dani's texts were "Wear pink tomorrow" or "Wear only silver earrings on Saturdays" or "Put your hair in braids Friday." Dani always called the shots for their group. She may not invite Rachel to her house anymore, but she still liked telling her what to do.

Tonight the text was from Maggie:

"Check your email! That Jeanie Blair is a worm! I'm so mad I could scream! Oh, and remember to ask your dad about Robin Heller!"

"What was it with worms today?" Rachel wondered. She grabbed her backpack and pulled out the flyer Mrs. Potter, the art teacher, had given them in art class. It read,

Let's Draw with Robin Heller.
Author of MUKLUK the Eskimo comic strip.
Don't miss this one-night-only opportunity!
Come join us at the Mucols building for a night that will change how you think about art.

26

Learn step-by-step directions for drawing
cartoons and caricatures.
Hear tips for making a living as an artist.
Must be accompanied by a parent.

Rachel wasn't going to miss this. She followed MUKLUK the Eskimo in the newspaper. Robin Heller was her favorite artist. She wanted to improve her art skills so maybe she could be an artist someday. She could do scenery, but people were more difficult, even if the girls at club had recognized Brian's face. The Mucols building was all the way across town. The flyer said you needed to be with a parent. She needed her dad to say yes to this. She wouldn't take no for an answer.

Rachel opened her email. She saw an email with an attachment from Tomas Blake. Tomas was a mystery. He acted smart and nice in class, but in the halls he was meaner than a mad toad in a pot of boiling water. Tomas had been suspended yesterday for fighting with a boy named Darren Marks. It was really nice not having him in class for a day. Tomas had never emailed her. She wouldn't consider him a friend. This was weird.

Rachel noticed that the entire class was copied on the email as well. The attachment was an attempt at a story by Jeanie, but it was terrible.

Rachel started reading about a dog and three goblins. Then it moved into short, rude excerpts about kids in their classes. She read an awful section about Wendy. Wendy didn't have a cell phone or Rachel would have texted her. Clearly, Jeanie liked to use alliteration as she had eight words in one sentence that started with W. Rachel fumed as she read on.

She read a recounting of Darren and Tomas's fight. Rachel had been in the cafeteria when that happened. Jeanie didn't have the details right at all. Tomas had been totally antagonizing Darren, not the other way around.

Her eyes widened as she came to the next paragraph. Her heart felt like it stopped. She saw her own name pop off the page. She read on feeling dread creep over her.

Rachel Landon rolled round the rim.
She really could use quite a trim.

28

Her butt fell flat
as she went kerplat.
I'm surprised she didn't break a limb.

Rachel was shocked. She knew she'd gained some weight since her mom's accident, but Jeanie hardly knew her. And here she was calling her fat and telling everyone about her embarrassing fall. And the girl couldn't write a limerick to save her life. The first two lines had eight syllables, but the last one had nine. They are all supposed to be the same. Plus, the third and fourth lines are supposed to have the same amount of syllables. Rachel chided herself. Who cared about poetry structure when this girl just criticized her and shared it with the whole school? Or Tomas did. Rachel wondered how he got it.

Rachel slammed down her phone on the couch beside her. "I'm going to be like Mrs. Keller and laugh it off. Ha-ha-ha," she said out loud to the empty room. But that didn't really work. Rachel continued to fume. She *was* mortified.

Rachel jumped when the microwave

beeped at her. She had forgotten all about eating. She washed her hands again and pulled out her dinner. She sat down on the couch and turned on the TV. She didn't usually watch it but welcomed the company. She grabbed her sketchbook and began sketching as she ate the plastic-tasting food. She drew Jeanie's face and then added fangs and pimples all over it. She pretended to be Robin Heller and turned Jeanie into a caricature. Her mind kept replaying the worm incident and the pathetic apologies.

Rachel still felt angry energy bursting within her. She tossed her sketchbook down and went to look for her paints. The cabinet by her dad's desk held her collection. She rummaged through the mess until she found them. She dropped the orange tube on her sweats, which reminded her of the stain on her jeans.

Rachel stood up and looked at the clock: 7:30 p.m. Where was he? Rachel started the wash to try to occupy her mind with something else. Maybe her dad would be home soon. She sat back by her sketchbook on the couch to watch one more show. Then she would pull her jeans out of the washer to air dry. She didn't realize she'd fallen asleep until she awoke to her dad collapsing beside her. Rachel looked at the clock: 11:45. "Why are you so late?" she asked through a yawn.

"Sorry, kiddo. Rough day at work, so a couple of us went out afterwards."

"Dad," Rachel said, becoming alert, "the artist Robin Heller is coming to do a special Let's Draw class in a few weeks. I need you to come with me or I can't go."

Her dad slapped her leg in his dismissive way. "*That* can be discussed tomorrow. Let's get ourselves to bed. I'm whipped."

Rachel slept fitfully that night. When she did sleep, she dreamed about worms flinging through the air at her. She woke up only to drift back into dreaming about things she could say to Jeanie. Why had Jeanie singled her out? Rachel vowed to make sure she would be sorry.

3 ~ The Sketch

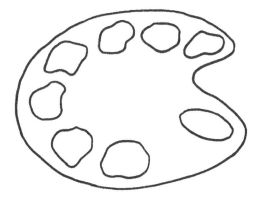

Rachel missed the blowup at school on Friday because Jeanie didn't show up until after lunch. Something about dentist appointments, she heard, was the reason. Rachel was in PE with Mr. Moore in a different wing of the school. She was so disappointed. It sounded like Darren had stormed down the hall ready to attack, but Mr. Bostrick stepped in, just in time. Mr. Bostrick was the school principal. He called Jeanie into his office after school, but no one knew her consequence.

It seemed like most of the kids forgot about the whole thing over the weekend. When Jeanie ended up absent Monday through Wednesday, it really was forgotten. Rachel couldn't forget, though, and fumed about Jeanie all week. When she saw Jeanie at school on Thursday, she decided she wouldn't be going to Character Club.

Rachel wished Dani had as short a memory as everyone else. Ever since Dani threatened Rachel to stay away from Brian, Dani hadn't eaten lunch with Maggie or Rachel. Laura also left them to sit with Dani. Every time Rachel caught a glimpse of Dani, Dani was glaring at her. Today it was through her designer glasses. What a fake. She didn't need glasses. What was going on with their group? Rachel knew Maggie's sensitive heart stressed about it daily.

That night Rachel's dad was actually home for dinner. He noticed Rachel's foul mood and asked about it. "You're usually so happy on Thursdays after Character Club. What gives?" Rachel felt a tinge of surprise that her dad would notice this. She still didn't feel like explaining about Dani or why, if she ever saw that Jeanie Blair again, she'd pull her hair out.

She didn't have to. Her dad's phone buzzed. He read a quick text and, blowing her a quick kiss, explained that he needed to get back to the office to "put a fire out."

"Dad, before you go," Rachel started to ask, "I really need to make sure you are home that Wednesday for Robin Heller's art class."

Her dad paused. "Sure. Of course. I'll get it on my calendar." His phone buzzed again. "Sorry, kiddo. Gotta run."

Rachel watched him rush out the door. She crossed the room to his desk and turned over an envelope. She picked up a black marker and wrote "Don't forget–Let's Draw." Rachel sighed and lumbered upstairs to her room. She pulled out her sketchbook and let her pencil lead her fingers. As her pencil moved back and forth, she noticed a garden beginning to take shape. It seemed familiar, but she sure didn't recognize it. Maybe she'd seen it on one of her walks home from school.

Rachel's vision clouded. She rolled over

on her back and blinked at the ceiling in perfect control of her tears. She'd stopped allowing tears around the time she noticed her dad doing the same. That's why the tears over her jeans last week had surprised her.

Rachel forced herself off the bed and walked down the hall toward what had been her parents' room. Dad always kept the door shut and never went in there anymore. Rachel went to look at the shelf above her dad's old antique cabinet. She overheard him brag that it once belonged to Benjamin Franklin's family.

A small clear box sat on the shelf above the cabinet; it held a dried boutonniere inside. Her dad had worn it on his wedding day. Beside it in a small vial was the one he'd worn at her mother's funeral. Rachel left the room to get away from the memories. Her stomach growled.

She wandered downstairs and into the kitchen to find a snack. She started some microwave popcorn as she flipped on the television for background noise. While she waited, Rachel decided to organize her supplies in the cabinet by her dad's desk.

Rachel tried to sort her pencils by color. When she finished with the reds, she picked up the oranges. She owned so many that they didn't quite fit in her hands. Instead of laying them aside, she tried to pick up one more. Her fingers just weren't long enough and the entire pile spilled out of her hands. They rolled down her leg, across the floor, and under her dad's desk. With exasperation, she collected the reachable ones, then ducked down to look under the desk. There were a few way back against the wall.

Rachel stared at them, as if trying to will them to roll toward her. She tried to muster the energy to crawl under there, knowing there would be cobwebs and dust bunnies. These gave her the willies. Rachel smelled something burning just as the microwave beeped. She raced into the kitchen. Too late. Rachel dumped the burnt popcorn kernels and washed her hands. Rachel sensed a frustrating energy building inside her.

Rachel trudged back upstairs to her room with her colored pencils. She flopped onto her bed to study her garden sketch, which was almost complete. It needed some color. She pulled out her green pencils and chose four to start coloring the leaves and stems.

With each stroke of color, she sensed her heart calming down. After she finished the greenery, she moved to the flowers. Each colored pencil seemed to know which flower to go to. Her garden began to glow with beautiful yellows, pinks, and deep oranges. Long, leafy variegated greens poked up amidst the colors. She longed to transport herself to this garden somehow. If only she knew where it was. Maybe it was heaven. Rachel wondered if her mom could see her from there. She thought about adding her mother to the picture but decided against it. Before she knew it, the clock read 11:00.

Rachel pulled out her phone and snapped a picture of the sketch. She may not be able to visit the actual garden, but now she could look at it anytime. She sank backward onto her pillow, exhausted.

Rachel dreamed that she was walking in that garden. Her mother was walking ahead of her. Rachel followed trying to catch up, but her mom kept fading into the mist. Someone brushed her hair out of her face, and gentle lips touched her forehead. Somehow her shoes came off. A blanket floated down from the sky and covered her body. She fell into a deep sleep.

When she woke up the next morning, she was still fully dressed except for her shoes. She could hear her dad snoring from the guest room next door.

In art class that day, Rachel looked at her watercolor piece. She had hoped to enter it into the art show contest. Learning to blend the colors had brought so much healing to Rachel's aching heart. Rachel completely forgot about asking her dad for the entrance fee of fifteen dollars. Maybe it was because she figured he'd say no anyway.

Mrs. Potter, the art teacher, walked up behind her and asked, "Will you be entering that in the contest, Rachel? I think it has a good chance of winning the two-hundred-dollar prize."

Rachel sighed and set the art down on

the table. "I don't have the money. I didn't get to ask my dad for it."

"Hmm," Mrs. Potter replied. "That's too bad. I wonder . . ." Her voice trailed off as she walked away. Mrs. Potter had trouble completing thoughts often.

Rachel shrugged and worked the rest of the period on the sketch for her sculpture idea. The kids at her table all twittered about Robin Heller's visit. Rachel joined the excitement. She couldn't wait to meet her perceived mentor. The bell rang and Rachel was about to walk out. Mrs. Potter called, "Rachel, please leave your watercolor on my desk."

Rachel obeyed and headed to her next class. She looked forward to working on fractions with Brian.

At lunch the next Monday, Dani and Laura parked themselves by Maggie and Rachel. They acted like last week never happened. Dani was full of questions. "So what's going on with Brian, Rach?" Dani quizzed her as soon as she sat down. She was wearing tight black jeans and a cold-shoulder blouse. She looked ready for the art show, not the lunchroom.

"I don't know." Rachel shrugged. "We've just been working together in math."

"Sounds like he wants some homework help. Betcha he asks this week. He probably needs to keep his grades up to play football," Dani predicted, as she bit the top off a potato fry with extra force.

Rachel furrowed her brow. She didn't know how to comment, so she stayed quiet.

The next day, Brian did ask her to stay after school in the library to do their homework together. Rachel agreed since Dani didn't seem angry anymore. They finished the homework in twice the time it usually took. It was so much fun though, Rachel felt it was worth it. She went home feeling sweet butterflies in her stomach.

By the time dinner was over, the butterflies weren't sweet anymore. Rachel silently thanked heaven that her dad was home. He took her temperature. "101.1!" he exclaimed. "No school for you tomorrow. I'll see if I can get off."

"No, Dad. I'll just lie on the couch and

sleep. You don't have to be here." Rachel tried to sound brave even though inside she wished he would stay home with her.

"Are you sure?" her dad asked.

"Yeah. I'll be fine."

The next morning Rachel didn't wake up until after 10:00 a.m. In the kitchen there was an instant oatmeal packet sitting next to a bowl and spoon, which Rachel's dad must have set out. Rachel smiled weakly at the gesture and began to heat up some water. Her head was throbbing, and she wished she hadn't shooed her dad off to work. Sick days made her ache for her mother's care. Her mom would have served bananas, rice, and toast all day with some ginger ale to wash it all down.

When the oatmeal was ready, Rachel made her way to the couch to eat. She didn't even wash her hands. She watched some TV between dozes. When she woke up enough to look at the clock, it was three thirty in the afternoon. She felt remarkably better.

Her dad walked in the door a few minutes later and announced, "I got off early so I can take care of you!"

Rachel sat up. "Thanks, Dad. I'm actually feeling so much better."

"Oh, that's good. I'll make you dinner. I stopped at the grocery store on the way home. How does soup sound?" He held up two cans with pride.

"Great, Dad." Rachel gave him a weak smile.

As her dad went into the kitchen, Rachel's phone buzzed with a text. It was from Dani.

"Missed U 2day. Hope U feel better. Pop quiz in history—study ch 3!"

That was super nice of Dani. After the nastiness of last week, Rachel was glad to have things back to normal. Rachel spent the remaining hours of the evening studying history. Her energy wasn't back to normal, but history wasn't her strongest subject. She was thankful to get to study for a quiz, instead of being surprised by it the next day. She only paused to eat the canned chicken noodle soup her dad made for her.

When Rachel walked into history class on Thursday, she expected her history teacher, Mr. Clymer, to hand her the pop quiz. Instead he just looked up and said, "Welcome back, Rachel."

Confused, she answered, "Thanks." She hesitated a moment waiting for the quiz, but he offered nothing. Rachel finally asked, "Did I miss a quiz yesterday?"

"No, ma'am." Mr. Clymer smiled, then asked, "Would you like me to give you one?"

"Uh, no thanks." Rachel continued, "I just thought . . ." Suddenly it dawned on her. Dani set her up. She looked to the back of the room and caught Dani's smirk as she whispered to Laura sitting across the aisle. Rachel fumed as she sat down in the front row as far away from them as she could get. So much for things being back to normal.

Rachel kept working with Brian in math class even when she could feel Dani's eyes trying to burn holes in Rachel's head. It felt gratifying to have attention from a boy and bug Dani at the same time.

Brian asked her to help him study in

the library again after school for the math test they had the next day. Rachel decided that was a much better option than Character Club—a club where people threw worms on her and invented nasty poems about her. She hid from Maggie when it was time to meet.

Friday's test went well. The computerized test doled out their scores immediately. Rachel earned a 92 percent, which was a little lower than usual. Brian earned an 84 percent. He let out a whoop that raised Mr. Bittel's eyebrows. Rachel didn't even see Dani enter the lunchroom that day as she and Brian celebrated his victory. But anyone who was paying attention would have noticed the daggers Dani's eyes shot at Rachel when she saw her.

The next Thursday, Wendy approached Rachel about missing her at Character Club. Rachel shrugged and said, "I don't want to have anything to do with that Jeanie Blair."

"Why not?" Wendy asked.

"Because of what she said about me. I can't believe you're not mad. She said bad things about you too."

Wendy snorted, "Oh, I was. But I forgave her."

"Why?"

"Because she's human just like me. On another day it could have been me caught saying or writing something bad about someone. It's a waste of time to stay angry at people. Besides, she apologized. I said I forgave her. So, I do. I hope you'll come back today."

Rachel did go back to club but not entirely of her own free will. Maggie waited outside Rachel's last class when the bell rang after school. She wouldn't let Rachel out of her sight and escorted her all the way to Mrs. Keller's house.

Once a month, Mrs. Keller arranged a service project for the kids to do. She felt strongly that giving back grew character. Apparently, last week she had told the kids to bring baked goods, bottled waters, or healthy snacks. They were going to make care packages for local police officers. Rachel felt empty-handed watching the other kids walk in with their items.

Maggie gasped, "Oops! I totally spaced

the service project!" She hit herself on the forehead with an open hand. "Duh! I guess I was too worried about making sure you got here!"

"Oh, so I'm your service project!" Rachel rolled her eyes at Maggie. Maggie may have the biggest heart of anyone she knew, but she tended to be a little flighty. "At least I'm not the only one who doesn't have anything," Rachel consoled.

Three baskets sat in Mrs. Keller's living room. All the drinks went in one basket. The homemade baked goods sat in another. The granola bars and other packaged items were piled in a third. Anything that didn't fit went into the corner for the club's ongoing collection for military families living abroad.

Mrs. Keller gave the empty-handed girls the job of wrapping the giant baskets with cellophane and tying huge bows around them. Angel and Wendy had also forgotten to bring something. They worked on the third basket.

Once all the baskets looked beautiful with their colorful ribbons, Mrs. Keller asked some boys to carry them out to her SUV.

Several other cars were lined up in front of Mrs. Keller's home. She never had any trouble finding volunteer drivers for their service projects.

Jeanie stood with her dad and Claire at the head of the car line. Claire was Jeanie's best friend. She was always bouncing those blonde curls around and seemed really cheerful. She reminded Rachel of Tigger the tiger. Rachel couldn't understand why Claire would want to hang out with Jeanie. Miss Jeanie-Meanie-Writes-Lies-About-Everyone. Rachel looked for another parent to ride with, but Jeanie ran over to her and Maggie just as Rachel spotted Ethan's mom.

"Oh Rachel, I'm so glad you're back. You are the only person I haven't had a chance to apologize to!" She paused to take a breath. "I'm so sorry for what I wrote about you in my story. It wasn't right at all, and I feel terrible that you saw it. Could you ever find it in your heart to forgive me?"

When worded that way, Rachel figured she could probably forgive her at some point. It just wouldn't be today. So she nodded.

"Oh, thank you!" Jeanie gushed, misunderstanding the meaning behind Rachel's nod. "Please ride with us!" Jeanie grabbed Rachel's hand and pulled her toward her dad's Jeep Grand Cherokee.

Jeanie climbed in the front with her dad. Rachel climbed in the back followed by Maggie, then Claire. Mr. Blair drove to the police station. The girls chattered away about past experiences with the police.

Maggie started with the time her mom got pulled over by a police officer and tried to get out of the fine. Her mom had rambled on and on about how it's impossible to focus on the speed limit with four kids in the van. The police officer just smirked and gave her the speeding ticket.

Jeanie remembered when she was in preschool. A police officer came to her house because an elderly neighbor had been driving dangerously. Her little dog Henry tried to attack him. The officer knelt down and offered his hand to Henry to sniff. Before the officer left, Henry was licking him all over the face like they were best friends.

Rachel smiled at the story. She wished she had a dog to keep her company at night when her dad worked. She would never suggest it, though.

Claire told a story about how she and her little sister had been separated from their parents at an outdoor fair. A nice police officer had let them sit with him on a bench until they were reunited with their parents.

Rachel remained silent. She didn't want to share the experience she was recalling—police officers diverting traffic while firefighters tried to extract her mother from their car. Rachel had flown out when it flipped and miraculously survived. Her mom was trapped inside, unconscious. She never woke up, not even to say good-bye. Rachel stared hard out the window trying to block out the other girls' chatter. She felt Maggie squeeze her right hand. Rachel squeezed back. She was so thankful that Maggie could read her mind.

The group arrived at the station and spilled out of the cars. Mrs. Keller led the way inside. Mr. Blair carried one of the baskets. Ethan and Lucas carried another. Cayden and

Peter fought over who would carry the third.

Inside, several officers awaited their arrival. Four men and one woman lined the corridor looking very sharp in their uniforms. Rachel was surprised to see the woman but intrigued about the idea of a female police officer. Maybe she could be a cop and an artist.

Once all the kids and parents crowded into the room, Mrs. Keller presented the three baskets. Her kind speech caused Rachel to ache over the weeks she had skipped coming to club. There was something soothing about just being near Mrs. Keller. The officers were delighted with the treats and thanked the clubbers profusely. Three of them collected the baskets and carried them out of the room.

One male officer stayed in the room and introduced himself as Officer Matthews. Rachel's eyes widened. He shared Brian's last name. She wouldn't forget that anytime soon. The female was Officer Sanders. The two of them led the kids on a tour of the facility. When they took them outside to see the patrol car, the boys went wild with questions. It took Mrs. Keller more effort than usual to quiet them down.

After the tour, Officer Matthews and Officer Sanders led the kids back inside to what looked like a gym. "This is where we teach small classes," Officer Matthews explained. "Officer Sanders is going to talk to you about self-defense."

The boys got excited again. Cayden air-karate-chopped Peter. Another boy grabbed Ethan around the neck and ruffled his long hair. Rachel looked nervously around the room. A few of the girls were snickering at the boys. She didn't like to think about being attacked. It sounded too scary. Mrs. Keller shushed them all so Officer Sanders could begin.

"It's best to avoid a confrontation in the first place. Use your head and avoid putting yourself in a potentially dangerous situation. Sometimes having a plan is the best protection. Go for a run with a group, instead of alone. Avoid less traveled paths or places. If using public transportation, choose full train cars or sit near the driver of a bus. Let your parents know your schedule. Carry a cell phone."

Rachel caught Jeanie out of the corner

of her eye. She elbowed her dad as if to say, "Told you I needed one." Even though it was nice to have a cell phone, Rachel would rather have her dad here to bug him for one.

Mrs. Keller thanked the officers for their time. Then she reminded the kids to say thank you. She herded the kids out to the parents' vehicles, and they all headed back to her house.

Maggie's mom was waiting in front of Mrs. Keller's house when they arrived. She looked frantic. She waved Maggie to the van yelling, "Hurry up! We're late to pick up your brothers!"

Rachel heard Megan moo at her as Maggie hugged Rachel before sprinting to her mother's van. Maggie jumped in the car as Megan announced, "Mommy, I need go boom boom."

Rachel heard Mrs. Walters groan as Maggie pulled the door shut. Rachel gave Meggie Moo a little wave.

Most of the kids dispersed quickly because so many parents were already there for the field trip. Rachel was about to start walking home when Mrs. Keller asked if she could show her something.

Rachel smiled at the opportunity to stay with Mrs. Keller. She followed her across the driveway to a patch of garden under the flagpole. It wasn't the one from her sketch, but it was beautiful. Mrs. Keller stared down at a section where there were a bunch of small green seedlings. She joked, "These are my nemeses."

Rachel didn't think they looked so terrible. "Why is that?"

Mrs. Keller continued, "All summer long these weeds keep poking up where they don't belong."

"They look a lot like that plant," Rachel said, pointing to the large green plant with little purple flowers.

"They are that plant. Offspring weeds."

Confused, Rachel asked, "How can baby plants be weeds?"

"A weed is anything that grows where you don't want it to. I need to get these out. Would you like to help?"

Rachel figured her dad would be working, so she relished the time with Mrs.

Keller. She smiled and said, "Just tell me what to do."

Mrs. Keller bent down and started digging with a small shovel. Rachel studied Mrs. Keller's shoulder-length hair as she dug under a small plant. It had a solo stripe of gray in it that you couldn't see when she was looking right at you.

Mrs. Keller pulled out the leaves in demonstration. Two stems came up in her hand. Then she gave Rachel the shovel and sat on her bench by the flagpole. "I don't have the back that I used to. I really appreciate your help, Rachel."

"Oh, I don't mind. I've got nothing to get home to." Rachel tried to dig out the weeds like Mrs. Keller showed her. She realized she'd been more focused on Mrs. Keller's hair than what she was doing in the garden but didn't want to ask for another demonstration. She didn't love touching the dirt.

"I've also been wanting to talk to you about the last time you were here. We've missed you the last two weeks."

Rachel reddened. It touched her that

Mrs. Keller would notice that she hadn't been there with so many other kids in Character Club. "Um, I was sick and then I had some tests to study for."

"Oh, well, I'm glad to hear it was just that. I was worried it might have had something to do with those worms."

Rachel swallowed. Mrs. Keller had a way of seeing right into your soul. She slowly admitted, "Well, maybe that too." She started digging a little faster.

"Or could it have been something I said?" Mrs. Keller tucked that gray strip of hair behind her ear.

"Something you said?" Rachel questioned, looking up. It was maybe something Jeanie said but never Mrs. Keller. Mrs. Keller was always so nice.

Mrs. Keller continued, "I didn't know about your mother. I'm so sorry that I suggested she wash your jeans. I had no idea she was gone."

Rachel wilted onto the grass. She dropped the shovel and hugged her legs.

Mrs. Keller joined Rachel on the grass.

She put an arm around her. "I hope you'll come back next week, Rachel. Our next topic may be able to soothe some of your pain."

4 ~ Sleepover

The next night, just about every girl from school met up at Valerie Ager's home for her sleepover birthday party. No one missed an event at the wealthy Ager estate. Valerie was an only child and lived with her dad, a butler, a cook, and a housekeeper.

Dr. Ager had been raised in Europe. When he met and married Valerie's mother, she insisted that they live in the States where she had been born. He brought his three favorite employees with him.

After a few short years of living this way, Valerie's mother decided she didn't want to be married nor even be a mother. She left him, Valerie, and all the "help" behind. Valerie didn't remember her at all. A framed picture of the woman sat in her room, but Valerie never talked about her. The cook seemed to be enough of a mother, and they were always whipping up new recipes together. Rachel wished there was a cook in her family to be like a mom to her.

When Mrs. Walters picked Rachel up, the only good-bye Rachel's dad gave her was a text from work:

"Don't drop your phone in the pool."

Mrs. Walters chatted excitedly about the party like she was going herself. She was dressed up in her nicest floral dress with a suede fringe vest. When they arrived at the Ager estate, the butler opened the sliding door for them. The girls climbed over Megan's little body. Marley was in the seat next to her. Maddox sat in the back with Rachel and Maggie. Maggie used her best manners to say, "Our bags are in the back, sir." The boys were impressed by his sharp uniform. Mrs. Walters giggled at him.

Megan said, "Is he gonna gib you ticket too, Mommy?"

Mrs. Walters's giggle disappeared. "He's a butler, not a cop. Shut the door, boys." She squealed off.

"Mom!" Maggie screamed and ran after her. "Our bags are still in there!"

The old van screeched to a halt. Rachel saw the kids' heads all slam forward, then back. The butler opened the back to retrieve the girls' bags. Megan was saying, "Is he called a butter because he has a big butt?"

Mrs. Walters's face turned the same color it had at Mrs. Keller's house, and she shushed Megan. Maggie looked at the butler and apologized for her sister's rude comment. He just laughed and said as he shut the back of the van, "I do like butter!"

Rachel could hear the boys' laughter as Mrs. Walters raced away. The butler ushered them through the mansion. They exited through large sliding glass doors to the huge backyard. The early fall air felt crisper out here. Jeanie, Claire, Wendy, and Angel had a game of pool volleyball going on. To the side, above a cascading waterfall that only fell about a foot, sat an oval-shaped hot tub. Valerie and a few other girls huddled inside it, warming up.

"Hey!" Valerie waved, genuinely happy to see them arrive. Most of the girls from their school were there, including Dani and Laura. Valerie's cousins from Denmark were there as well.

Maggie and Rachel rushed to change in the "pool house," as Valerie's dad called it. They dumped their clothes on a chaise lounge and jumped in the pool to join the volleyball game.

After a while Ms. Olsen, the cook, came out and announced that dinner was ready. The girls all scrambled out of the pool and toweled off. They knew and appreciated Ms. Olsen's gourmet spreads. For the next hour, they feasted on apple-roasted pork, sausages, potatoes, rye bread, and various cheeses. She also managed to throw in some American food. She had tortilla chips complete with a homemade salsa. Her seven-layer bean dip was the hit of the night, though, and had the girls scraping the bowl clean.

Once they had eaten their fill, Ms. Olsen told them to head inside to the game room until dessert was ready. Several girls sat down at a beautiful wooden table to play board games. Rachel headed for the ping-pong table to see if Maggie would take her on. Before Rachel had crossed the room, Claire called out, "Hey, everyone! Let's play Around the World!" She bounced over to the table.

Several girls came to join her, and they soon had five girls on each side. Rachel and Maggie lined up with Claire, Jeanie, and Angel. Dani and Laura got behind Valerie, Amanda, and Wendy.

Claire served the ball to Valerie, dropped her paddle, and ran to the back of Valerie's line. Valerie easily hit it back over, dropped the paddle, and ran to the other side. Rachel picked up her paddle just in time to whack a bad shot over the net. Too far over the net. Dani put her hands up like she was being shot at so as not to hit the ball on accident. Rachel was out, but

Dani was the one looking furious.

Rachel sat down on a cozy-looking couch to watch the game play out. She tried not to pay attention to Dani staring her way and whispering something to Laura. Dani wasn't even trying to hide that her comments were directed at Rachel.

One by one the girls were eliminated. Three hits was the highest volley. Laughter about the lack of skill in the room permeated the air. They were all good sports as they were eliminated. The game always passed quickly. Claire plunked down beside Jeanie when she couldn't pick up the paddle in time to hit the ball, because Wendy forgot to put it down after her turn.

Finally it was down to Valerie and Angel. Each girl had to hit the ball, lay down her paddle, and spin around before picking it back up to make the return. They both spun three times before Valerie hit the game-ending shot. The best volley so far. Angel thought Valerie's hit was going to be long, but it nipped the edge of the table. The birthday girl was proclaimed the winner.

"Good game!" Valerie beamed. "Everybody back in!" she called, motioning her hands for the girls to start a new game.

Rachel decided just to watch. Plenty of other girls who had been spectators for the first round took her place. The girls played for about an hour before Ms. Olsen came in to announce, "Dessert is ready!"

The girls panted heavily from the intense game as they headed down the corridor. It led to a long table covered with all sorts of amazing treats, including fruit salads, custards, and crepes. Some were on cake stands and others on fancy plates, creating different heights of displays on the table.

Rachel stacked her plate high with delicacies. She followed some girls down the winding staircase to the theater for the movie. The rest weren't far behind. They brought plates piled equally high to keep their mouths busy during the movies.

Valerie's dad had converted the basement into a makeshift theater complete with seating for about twenty people. He used it for "premiering" his movies that he made as a hobby. He created a lot of This Is Your Life–type films. Then he invited small groups of people to screen them on his colossal TV.

The girls filled every seat and a few settled in on the floor. There were plenty of beanbags to keep them comfortable. After a few movies, several girls had already fallen asleep. The others decided to settle in for the night.

They climbed the stairs and went down the hall that led to Valerie's wing. Her cousins went in one room with some of the girls who'd been hanging out with them. The rest lined up their sleeping bags on the floor in Valerie's gigantic room. Valerie, Amanda, and Maria climbed into her king-sized bed. Then Dani and Laura joined them. Rachel thought that seemed a bit assuming. Valerie, Amanda, and Maria were inseparable; since when did Dani and Laura even hang out with them?

There were several hushed conversations going on around the room. Rachel and Maggie formed a group with the other Character Club girls. They imagined what it would be like to live here all the time. Rachel didn't participate much. She was distracted by the whispers of the girls coming from the giant bed.

One by one the conversations quieted and heavy breathing took their place. Rachel couldn't get comfortable on the floor, so she kept turning over and over, attempting to fall asleep.

Then suddenly, she heard a brrrumpfh come from somewhere in the room. She sat up to look around and heard it again. Brrruumpfh. Her eyes widened. It was coming from the bed. It happened again. She covered her mouth to keep from laughing out loud. Rachel got on her knees to try to identify the perpetrator. The moonlight shining in from the window illuminated the five figures.

Rachel knew Laura was on the edge. Dani was second from the left. She heard it again. Dani was totally passing gas in her sleep! She turned to her other side to see if Maggie heard it. Maggie's rhythmic breathing convinced Rachel she was asleep. She scanned the whole room in the dim light. It didn't look like anyone was awake but her.

Brrruumpfh. It happened again. This

time Laura sat straight up in the bed. Her eyes met Rachel's. Both girls covered their mouths to keep from laughing as they stared at each other. Dani let another one loose, and Laura leapt from the bed like she'd been shot. Rachel couldn't hold in her laughter much longer. She watched as Laura grabbed her phone to capture a video when Dani let another one rip.

Rachel knew no one would recognize Dani in the dim light, but the thought was too funny to hold in any longer. Rachel scrambled out of her sleeping bag to escape to the bathroom down the hall where she could laugh out loud. Laura chased behind her.

Rachel had only used the outdoor bathroom earlier and couldn't remember which door it was. Laura was in the same predicament. The first door they checked opened into a beautiful personal library. The girls slipped into the room and burst out laughing.

It was not a huge room. Rachel guessed it to be the size of her room at home. But it had high ceilings and she counted nine rows of shelves. Straight ahead of her was a marble fireplace with ornate, bronzed-leaf patterns on each side. The bookshelves were made of a dark cherrywood. There was a matching ladder attached to a pole near the top shelf. The pole wrapped around three sides of the room. She walked over to the ladder in the back right corner and started sliding it along the pole. Wheels hidden in the ornate decoration at the bottom helped it glide along the track.

Laura jumped on the bottom rung as Rachel pushed it all the way around past the door they had come in. Three more rows of books were displayed above the door frame. The girls giggled together like old times.

Rachel stopped at the back left corner and sat on the L-shaped leather bench in front of the fireplace. Laura joined her and pulled out her phone. "Let's watch the video."

The girls leaned in close to each other to watch what Laura captured. The dim light made it hard to see anything, but the sound was unmistakable. The girls collapsed into each other to stifle their laughter.

Laura sat up and said, "I'll text it to you."

Rachel nodded and allowed her eyes

to take in all the books around the room. Some were modern stories she recognized, but there were many old classics with gold foil embroidery on the spines.

Laura interrupted her thoughts, "Wouldn't it be cool to have this in your house? I'd love to have this library, but I'd never read any of the books." Suddenly, Laura leapt up from the bench. She exclaimed, "Let's write a story." It didn't matter that it was the middle of the night. Laura crossed the room. There was a small decorative table with a little drawer. She slid it open and found what she'd been hoping to find: several sheets of paper and some pens. She grabbed one of each, plus a hardcover picture book of golf courses from around the world. Laura sat down cross-legged on a matching green couch and began to write, using the golf book as a desk.

"Come help me, Rachel. This will be fun." Rachel crossed the room and sat beside her. She watched as Laura scrawled out the scene that had just unfolded.

As all the wannabe princesses dreamed of

richer things, one of them had consumed too much of the infamous bean dip. Her gas-passing in her sleep had the volume of a gunshot in an echo chamber. The prince startled awake and entered the room of maidens who were all hoping to turn his head. The damsel Dani succeeded with a loud brrruumpfh, which she let loose as he walked past. He turned toward her, appalled by the horrible smell.

Laura stifled her laughter as she wrote but was becoming sleepy. Rachel was giggling beside her until she realized this was exactly what she was so angry at Jeanie for doing to her. She sobered at the thought.

Laura folded the paper, returned the pen, and took one last look at the luxurious library. Rachel noticed the chandelier had two rows of little lamps each with its own little red shade.

"Someday I'll have one of those in my library," Laura whispered as she backed out the door and let Rachel shut it. They tiptoed down the hall and back into Valerie's room. Rachel watched Laura tuck the paper into her pillow before crawling back into the bed. She didn't feel good about everything Laura wrote, but it sure felt good to have her friend back.

The next morning after a phenomenal breakfast, the girls started peeling off a few at a time as their rides arrived. Rachel and Maggie waited at the breakfast table with all five occupants of Valerie's bed from the night before. Rachel wasn't sure how she'd ended up by Dani, but she pretended things were fine. Dani commented while yawning that her stomach hurt a little bit. Rachel bit her lip to keep from smiling and glanced at Laura. Laura seemed to have missed the comment.

"Do you want some peppermint?" Valerie offered. "It's good for the stomach."

Dani opened her mouth to reply as the doorbell rang. The girls could see through the glass in the door that it was Dani's older brother. "Thanks, but I'm sure I'll be fine once I get home." She collected her things and walked out the door to her brother, without saying good-bye.

Rachel leaned over to whisper to Maggie what Dani had been doing in the night.

She was interrupted by Dr. Ager calling into the room, "Maggie, your mother is here for you and Rachel." They each gave Valerie a hug and gathered their things, thanking Dr. Ager as they left the mansion.

"How was the sleepover?" asked Mrs. Walters once they were on their way; she was much more subdued from the night before. Megan was asleep in her car seat. The boys were at soccer practice.

"A–ma–zing!" Maggie commented. The girls recapped the party events for Maggie's mom. Rachel left out her nighttime adventure with Laura.

It would be several hours before she realized her phone was missing.

5 ~ Betrayal

Monday morning Rachel headed to school feeling better than she had for weeks. Dani may not be her friend anymore, but it felt good to have Laura back. Even though she never found her phone all weekend, her dad never asked about it. She had enjoyed being out of touch. No texts. No Dani drama. Just quiet. She woke up feeling refreshed. She even had extra time to braid her hair. She felt a joyous rebellion doing it on a Monday knowing Dani would disapprove.

When Rachel entered the school building, Maggie came running up to her questioning, "Are you okay? I can't believe Laura did that! I texted you eighty thousand times last night! Wait. Why are you in braids? It's headband day."

Rachel gave her a confused look, and Maggie realized she didn't know. "Where have you been? It's all over social media!"

"I lost my phone after the party. I need to ask Valerie if I left it at her house," Rachel explained.

Maggie handed Rachel her phone. "This hit last night."

Rachel read a text containing most of Laura's story. Only Dani's name had been replaced with hers! Guys walked by making armpit noises at her. "Way to go, Rachel!" one said, laughing.

Rachel ignored them. "At least she didn't post the video."

A sick look crossed Maggie's face. "You know about it? It's right here." Maggie swiped up to another page. There was the video with Rachel's name plastered across the bottom.

Rachel's eyes narrowed in anger. "I don't know what I'm going to do about this, but something has to be done." She looked down the hall to see Laura laughing with Dani while Dani put on some bright lipstick using her locker mirror. Rachel headed straight for her.

As she walked by, a boy pointed and said, "Oh no, Rachel. There's a rip in your jeans! Wonder how it got there?"

Rachel grimaced and picked up her pace. "What is this all about?" Rachel demanded, waving Maggie's phone in Laura's face.

Laura looked at Rachel with a smirk. "Oh, Rachel. Don't be so sensitive."

Rachel's mouth dropped to the floor. "You posted this fake story and video about me when we both know who it really was and you want *me* not to be so sensitive?" Rachel could feel the heat rising in her face.

Dani broke in and said, "Oopsie," giving Rachel a bright red fake pout. "I guess now the whole school thinks it was you. I feel so sorry for you, Rachel. Oh, but I found your phone at the party." She paused to pull Rachel's phone out of her designer purse. She plopped it into Rachel's hand, shut her locker, and clipped away. Laura followed in her matching headband without even a glance backward.

Rachel hung her head and wondered what the day would have in store for her. Her reputation seemed ruined. She leaned against a locker. Maggie leaned on the one next to it and pulled the headband out of her hair. She dropped it in her backpack. She studied Rachel and quickly braided her hair to match. Rachel gave Maggie a weak smile and a hug. "Thanks."

Maggie hugged her back, "Guess I better get to class. See you at lunch."

Rachel watched Maggie walk down the hall thankful to have such a loyal friend. She looked down at her phone. One click of the button revealed she had 157 texts. She'd never been so popular. So much for the freedom of the weekend. She trudged to class without even reading a single one.

Rachel slumped down in a new chair across the room from Dani. She glanced over at Brian who was looking straight ahead. At least he wasn't making fun of her. She tried not to pay attention to the backward glances and half-hidden giggles from the other students.

Rachel felt a tug on her braid. She swung around ready to slap the culprit and saw Lucas with his hands up in surrender.

"Sorry! I was just trying to get your attention," Lucas whispered.

"Well, so is everyone today," she snapped.

"I wanted to let you know that I think what Laura did was stupid. Try not to let it get to you."

Rachel softened. "Thanks, but it already has."

He gave her a reassuring smile. "It'll pass in no time, don't worry."

Rachel gasped at his words.

Lucas' eyebrows shot up as he realized the double meaning in his words. "I didn't mean it that way! Honest. I'm sorry. I meant the teasing. That'll pass. They'll get bored. I wasn't trying to pick on you too. That's not me."

"Thanks, Lucas." Rachel chose to believe him. He had never been cruel before.

Rachel remembered he actually gave her a sympathetic pat on the back the day Peter and Cayden threw the worms on her. She smiled at him.

Mr. Bittel began his lesson on ordering fractions on the number line. The rest of class raced by quickly. Lucas partnered with Rachel during practice time. When the bell rang, a bunch of boys commented as they passed Rachel.

"Wanna eat lunch with me today, Rach? I have baked beans!"

"I hear gas is at an all-time low price today."

Rachel's face turned red as she gathered her things at a snail's pace while the room cleared out. When she finally stood up, Lucas was by her side. "I'll walk you to lunch," he smiled.

Rachel gave him a weak smile back. The two walked down the almost deserted hall to the lunchroom. When they entered, faithful Maggie was right inside. "There you are! I was getting worried. Hi, Lucas. Wanna sit with us?"

Lucas shrugged and headed toward the

lunch line. Rachel kept her head down as they followed Lucas and bought their lunch. They sat in a different area of the lunchroom than normal. Ethan joined them. Rachel tried to ignore all the noises coming from the boys all around her. It was obvious they were directed at her, though. One boy even turned and said, "Hey, Rachel, I have some cheese. Can you cut it for me?" He gave her a wink.

Trying to find a lighter side, Rachel commented, "Well, I guess I finally have all the boys' attention."

Maggie shot milk out of her nose as she laughed. "Ew!" Rachel half gagged, half laughed at her friend. Lucas snickered too. Soon the four of them were laughing so hard, it didn't matter what the rest of the room was doing. They didn't notice.

That night when Rachel arrived to the usual empty house, she turned on her phone to work through the list of texts. There were at least ten from Maggie. So many of them were numbers she didn't even know. She began deleting them without even reading them, especially when the first few words were "Let'r rip!" or "Pass that gas!" She noticed that there wasn't one from Dani telling her to wear a headband.

Rachel gave up after sifting through about half of them. She texted her dad that it was two days until the Let's Draw art class. An hour later she went to bed feeling betrayed and abandoned.

On Tuesday Rachel was surprised how much the incident really did seem to blow over. No one seemed to care that much anymore. No one except maybe Brian. He hadn't looked at her or talked to her since Friday.

That night at home Rachel sorted through the second half of texts on her phone. She found a text sent to Brian. She didn't even know she had his number. It said,

"Stay away from me. I don't want to help you with your math. Pay attention in class for a change."

Rachel was shocked. Dani must have sent it when she had her phone. Talk about a real worm.

Rachel jumped when the power went out suddenly. She sat in complete darkness. The silence was eerie. She started counting to keep herself calm. She tried to remember where the fuse box was. Just as she gathered the courage to go find it in the dark, the power came back on. "That was weird," she thought to herself.

On Wednesday morning not a comment was made about the video story. Maybe life could return to normal. Rachel wanted to explain to Brian what happened, but the announcements started. Each morning students from the film club recorded videos for teachers to play at their convenience. Rachel was only half paying attention until she heard a student reporter mention Dani's name.

"We want to thank Danielle Davis for this enlarged photograph her family is donating to the school. Dani drew the original sketch for the art show coming up in a few weeks," the student read.

Rachel looked up to see the other student holding up an eleven-by-fourteen matted and framed photo of her garden sketch! "But how?" she wondered. Then she remembered that Dani had her phone ALL weekend! How stupid. Why had she given that girl her passcode?

She rehashed all of Dani's offenses. First, Dani changed Laura's story to humiliate Rachel. Then, she texted Brian pretending to be her. Now, she's stealing her artwork. That was the final straw. She went to her photos folder to look at her picture of the sketch. It was gone.

Before lunch Rachel had a chance to confront Dani alone. Dani was at her locker in the hallway near the lunchroom. Rachel rushed up to her before she lost her nerve. "How dare you steal my sketch and try to pass it off as your own!"

Dani looked up at her and darted her painted eyes around to see who was paying attention. "I don't know what you are talking about, Rachel."

"You know you didn't draw that sketch," Rachel hissed.

"I created a print for the school. It'll

look great hanging by the office with *my* name on it. You should try to make something for the school too, Rach, instead of whining to me."

"What is *wrong* with you?" Rachel asked in frustration. "Why are you trying to ruin my reputation and everything I care about? What did I do to you?" Rachel's voice was getting higher. She was afraid it would crack and betray the wounds she was trying to hide.

"I told you to stay away from Brian Matthews. *You* should have listened," she snarled. Dani spun on her too-tall-for-school heels and sped down the hallway.

Rachel stood alone, stunned, in the passageway. "You won't get away with this!" Rachel called after her. "I have the original!" Rachel noticed Dani's step falter ever so slightly, but she kept going. Rachel didn't feel hungry. She walked away from the lunchroom toward the office. There, sitting on the floor inside the office was the framed picture of her sketch. A small gold label was mounted on the lower right corner which read "A Gift from Danielle Davis."

Anger surged inside her. None of the school secretaries were in the office at the moment. Rachel felt something come apart inside her. She bolted in and grabbed the picture. She ran outside through the nearest door which led around the corner to the garbage. She lifted the print over her head. Without thinking she heaved it toward the dumpster. Glass shattered, jolting her out of her rage. What had she done? She stood frozen for a second before she realized she needed to get out of there. Rachel backed away from the dumpster. She reached the door, but it had locked behind her. She was stuck outside. Rachel hoped no one had heard the shattering glass.

A younger boy, who looked a lot like Jeanie, bolted out the door, late for his PE class. He clutched a soccer ball under his arm. He raced toward two other boys who looked exactly like him. Rachel shook her head. She must be losing it. She was seeing double. No, triple. Rachel grabbed the door before it shut again and snuck back into the school. She crept into the lunchroom hoping no one noticed what she'd done.

But someone had.

During her last class, Rachel was called to Mr. Bostrick's office. He was known for being strict but reasonable. It was always better to visit him for winning a contest than for being in trouble. Rachel didn't have any experience with either.

As Rachel entered the office, Ms. Moss—Mr. Bostrick's secretary—gave her a dissatisfied look. "Have a seat, Rachel. Mr. Bostrick will be with you in a moment." His door was closed and she could hear voices inside. They were muffled but familiar. When at last the door opened, Laura and Dani emerged. Rachel fumed. Of course, Dani probably followed her down the hall and watched the whole thing.

Mr. Bostrick followed them out and motioned Rachel to come in. Dani sneered at Rachel as she passed her. Rachel stood and entered Mr. Bostrick's office behind him. He turned to look at her. "Do you know why you were called down here, Miss Landon?"

Rachel wasn't going to offer what she did just in case that wasn't the reason, so she timidly said, "No?"

"Was that a statement or a question?" Mr. Bostrick countered.

"Statement?" she questioned again.

"I've known you since kindergarten. You are not the type of student to damage property, Rachel. Please tell me what happened." His tone had softened.

Rachel desperately wanted to hold it together. She definitely didn't want to rat out Dani because she knew that would cause more trouble. Her heart raced inside her chest. She was sure Mr. Bostrick could see it beating through her shirt. What could she say? She couldn't think of a thing and sat there in silence. She studied her fingers in her lap.

Finally Mr. Bostrick cleared his throat. She looked up at him tentatively. He began, "Well, if you won't defend yourself, I have to give you a consequence after school. I can't even tell you that it's your word against Dani's because we have surveillance cameras. Rachel, this is so uncharacteristic of you. I'm disappointed. I believe there is more you aren't telling me, but if you won't speak, you leave me no choice. Have you heard of restorative justice?"

Rachel shook her head.

He continued, "You've destroyed school property, so you will attend to our school property. Your punishment will fit the crime. There are a few other students who will be joining you. Please report to Mr. Tom's office after school."

Mr. Tom was the building facilitator. He was funny and not your average custodian. He seemed to know how to fix things before they broke. He always showed up with a mop right when someone puked. It was like he knew it would happen before it did. All the kids thought he was fantastic. Many parents mistook him for the principal.

After school Rachel saw Maggie before heading to Mr. Tom's room. Maggie glared at her. "How could you do that to Dani's picture? I know what she did was mean, but destroying her picture crossed the line!"

Rachel was shocked that Maggie was

siding with Dani. She opened her mouth to try to explain.

Maggie spun on her heel and left Rachel standing there. Rachel had never felt so alone. Maggie was her rock. When life's waves crashed over Rachel, Maggie had always been there for her, as long as she could remember. Rachel watched her friend storm away as the storm inside her grew. She figured she had better get to her assignment before Mr. Tom got angry too. Then she realized Robin Heller's class was today! Rachel had completely forgotten about it. She sent a quick text to her dad.

"Dad, I have to stay after school. Pick me up at school instead of home at 4:30 or we won't make it to Robin Heller's Let's Draw class."

Inside Mr. Tom's small office sat a couple of students. Tomas was one of them. Peter from Character Club was another. The scene from the day he threw worms on her replayed in her mind. Rachel grinned at the poetic justice of Peter doing community service. She hoped it had something to do with worms. Maybe he would have to pull weeds.

Mr. Tom looked up at Rachel with a surprised look. "Well, you are one of the last people I ever expected to see here, but your name is on the list. You can hang with the boys until our last student arrives."

Rachel looked around the small office. It looked more like a workshop. Shelves lined the walls from floor to ceiling, all loaded with tools. Metal cabinets stood in between the shelves. Mr. Tom had set up a long workbench with cork board behind it. Tools hung from hooks in the board. As her eyes made their way around the room and back to the door, in walked Jeanie.

Mr. Tom looked up at her and said with a smile, "Ah! Here's our last helper. Another mysterious case." Rachel gulped. She didn't want to have to do community service with her.

Mr. Tom explained to the group that he had come up with two projects for them to complete before they could be dismissed. The boys' bathroom stalls needed to be repainted due to graffiti. Mr. Tom glanced at Peter while he spoke. Rachel caught that Peter was the perpetrator on that one.

"We'll have you two boys do that," he said, looking at Tomas and Peter. "Jeanie and Rachel, I'll have you two come with me to the art room."

Rachel felt a bit of a panic rise up within her. She hadn't forgiven Jeanie for the things she wrote. The thought of having to work side by side with her made Rachel feel a little shaky.

Mr. Tom gave each of the students some of the paint supplies to carry to the boys' bathroom. He asked Rachel and Jeanie to wait in the hall while he took Tomas and Peter inside to explain technique.

Then Mr. Tom came out of the bathroom and clapped his hands together in a tight clap. "Alright, you two. Onward march!" He laughed at himself and pointed one arm down the hall as if directing them for the first time.

It was impossible not to be happier after any interaction with Mr. Tom. He truly found joy in taking care of their school. The threesome made their way to the art room.

Once inside, Rachel saw their project. Piled high on a table was student artwork for the art show. Next to the artwork there was a pile of foam board in different colors. Several bottles of glue were laid out on the table as well.

"So, you two lucky ladies get to mount all these projects onto those boards. This is really going to help Mrs. Potter. She will be delighted," Mr. Tom explained.

The pile looked huge. Rachel couldn't believe how many submissions had been entered. A small pile that had already been mounted sat on Mrs. Potter's desk. Rachel worried she'd be here until dark, even if she did love art.

Mr. Tom must have caught her look because he added, "Just work until the late bus comes. If you don't get finished by then, someone else will complete the job."

Rachel knew that meant he would have to do it. Mr. Tom already did so much for the school. She decided that she'd work as fast as she could to try to complete the whole pile.

Mr. Tom left the two of them alone.

Jeanie vocalized her thoughts. "We can't let Mr. Tom do this. Let's figure out a system and get it done as fast as we can."

Rachel agreed and they set to work. They matched up each piece of art with a matte board. They fell into the rhythm of Jeanie spreading the glue and Rachel adhering the artwork. Rachel smoothed it into place once it was attached.

After several pieces, Rachel got up the nerve to ask, "So what'd you do to earn this work detail?"

Jeanie snorted. "I got caught sneaking out of that new substitute's class. One of my little brothers was out in the hall crying, so I wanted to check on him. She's no ordinary sub."

Rachel grinned. She knew Mrs. Murray well. She'd been substituting for Ms. Warber, their language arts teacher, for a while now and that woman didn't miss a thing. Ms. Warber sure was missing a lot, though. Rachel wondered what happened to her. She'd been out for weeks with no explanation.

"How many brothers do you have?"

Rachel asked.

Jeanie snorted again. "Three! And it's three too many! Triplets. I'm working on caring for them better, though. That's why I wanted to check on Barton when I heard him crying."

"I think I saw one of them outside today. He was running to PE with a soccer ball."

"That would be Ben." Jeanie smiled, then asked Rachel what she had done. Rachel explained about the shattered frame. Jeanie was impressed. "That's some serious snapping!"

"Huh?" Rachel questioned.

"You snapped. Here you are, a totally nice girl who just snapped for a minute and did something totally out of character. I'm guessing you don't normally go around breaking things?"

"No, I don't."

"Rachel, I don't normally go around writing mean things about people. I hope you can believe me. I can tell you are still angry with me."

Rachel changed the subject. "Are you going to Robin Heller's Let's Draw class tonight?"

"Oh, yes. I can't wait to meet her. I've read all her comics."

"I wonder what she's like?" Rachel mused.

"I bet she's hysterical. Probably cracking jokes every minute after writing cartoons all day long." Jeanie laughed. "Did you see the one where the bear is chasing Mukluk and they come to the sign that says 'Slow School Zone' and both stop running to walk through it? Then the bear continues chasing him when another sign says 'Resume Speed'? That one is so funny."

Rachel nodded and grinned. They talked about school and Character Club. They actually finished with five minutes to spare. They walked back down to Mr. Tom's office, tired but satisfied.

When Mr. Tom saw them, he exclaimed, "Fabulous! I kept an eye on your things. You are free to go. Come back and help anytime!" He gave them a wink. As nice as Mr. Tom was, Rachel didn't want to have to stay after school to work for him again—even if Jeanie wasn't so bad after all.

Jeanie and Rachel picked up their backpacks and headed outside. The late bus would pick up Jeanie any minute. A few other students stood around the flagpole waiting as well. Jeanie whispered, "Can I see your garden sketch? The one Dani stole?"

Rachel shrugged and pulled out her sketchbook. She handed it to Jeanie, open to the right page.

"Wow!" Jeanie exclaimed. "This is amazing. You are so talented."

Rachel beamed with pride at Jeanie's praise. If only she could get her dad's attention to look at her drawings too. The bus pulled around the corner.

Before Rachel could stop her, Jeanie flipped back a page. There staring back at her was her own face with fangs and pimples. "Oh," Jeanie said with a startled voice.

Rachel grabbed the book, hoping Jeanie didn't recognize herself. Jeanie looked at Rachel. "Don't worry about it. I deserve that." Jeanie walked to the bus with the other kids.

Rachel watched Jeanie climb on and slump into a seat. She felt an overwhelming sense of guilt. Wendy's words came back to her: "On another day it could have been me caught saying or writing something bad about someone."

Wendy was right. She immediately hoped Jeanie could be more forgiving than she had been so far.

6 ~ Red Card

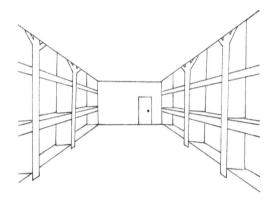

Rachel waited on the bench by the flagpole for her dad to arrive. She pulled out her phone and saw that he had never responded to her text. She texted him again.

"I'm ready. Please hurry! By the flagpole."

Rachel calculated how long it would take to get to the Mucols Center from the school. It would only be a few minutes longer than from home. Where was he?

While she waited, football practice ended. Some of the boys ran and jumped on the bus while others found their parents in the parking lot. Rachel saw Brian walk around the corner. He didn't get on the bus and didn't seem to have a ride waiting. He was walking right toward her bench. His eyes shifted, and then he stopped short and leaned against the flagpole.

Rachel looked at him and blurted out, "That text wasn't from me. Dani stole my phone and sent it pretending to be me."

Brian looked at her with surprise. "That sounds like a Dani move." As the truth dawned on him, he grinned. "So can we still work on math together?"

Rachel grinned back. "I guess so. Lucas is a pretty good partner, though."

"Yeah, I'm sure he's smarter than me." Brian smiled. "But if he's ever willing to share you . . ." He let his voice trail off, then asked, "How come you're still here?"

"Oh, I'm waiting for my dad to pick me up for Robin Heller's Let's Draw class. I had to work in the art room after school. Are you going?"

"No. All the classes in the world couldn't make me a good artist." A dark Suburban pulled around the corner. Brian said, "There's my ride. See you in math tomorrow."

Rachel sat on the bench alone for thirty more minutes. No text. No dad. And now there would be no art class. Rachel didn't even know what to think. How could he have forgotten? Rachel's stomach started to rumble. She pulled herself up and started the walk home. She didn't even bother texting her dad to tell him she was leaving the school.

As she walked home, she decided to sit across the street from her favorite house. The neighbors had a brick wall that was the perfect height for sitting on. She found a granola bar when she pulled out her sketchbook. Rachel penciled in the porch and some of the pots as she munched on it. She focused on the white pillars for a while before turning back to the flowers. The sun was sinking behind her casting a golden hue on everything. She wished she had her colored pencils with her. She kept sketching until dusk turned the golden hues into grays across the street.

Rachel packed up and started walking home. Once the sun set, it got dark fast. She pulled out her phone and used its flashlight. When she was still a few blocks away, she thought she heard footsteps behind her.

She turned around but didn't see anyone. She picked up her pace. She heard them again. Fear began to creep into Rachel's mind. She heard Officer Matthews's voice telling her not to put herself in a potentially dangerous situation. She hadn't thought ahead at all. She wasn't in the worst part of town, but she shouldn't be out walking alone after dark. This street had very few houses on it and backed up to the shopping center. It felt like she had broken every rule of advice he'd given. She did have her cell phone, but if someone was following her she wasn't going to stop and text her dad now. She should have texted him when she left the school. She walked faster. She strained to hear footsteps, but her heart was racing too loudly in her chest.

Rachel turned a corner. She glanced back to see if she could see someone back there.

Shadows lurked everywhere. She couldn't be sure. She increased her pace again. At her own corner, she burst into a run. She raced all the way to her driveway where her dad was getting out of his car.

Gasping for breath, she ran right into him and began beating her fists on his chest. "You forgot me! I missed my art class! I waited forever! I thought someone was chasing me. What if something happened? What is wrong with you? Where were you?"

Her dad peeled her off his chest. "Not everything is about you, Rachel." He turned and stormed into the house.

Rachel threw down her backpack. Anger replaced her fear. She yelled after him, "I hate you!" Her dad didn't return.

After school the next day, Maggie took off for Character Club with Angel and Wendy leaving Rachel alone. Rachel followed Jeanie and Claire who were walking with some boys. She wasn't even sure why she was going. It must have been Mrs. Keller's comment from last week. Maybe this would be exactly what she needed. She felt like her whole world was crumbling around her. She definitely didn't want to go home in case her dad was there. But then again, why would he be?

When Rachel walked in, she saw that Valerie had brought all the leftover food from her birthday party. No one seemed to care that it was from the weekend. They were all piling plates high with treats because Mrs. Keller usually only served healthy fruit and protein snacks.

When Rachel got through the snack line and outside, she stopped in her tracks. Across the patio behind the couches, Mrs. Keller's garden bloomed in all the colors from her sketch. She set her plate on a ledge and headed toward it. Rachel knelt down by the garden.

Rachel reached out and touched a purple-and-yellow flower. Its petals were so soft. She wished she knew the names of them all. There were yellow and orange ones; others in reds, purples, yellows, and fuchsias. There were even mini ones striped with different colors. Rachel breathed deeply and smelled sweet floral scents.

The scene captivated Rachel and she felt a calm she didn't understand. Her mind must have noticed this garden before today because she had sketched it. Her conscious mind never realized it.

Rachel sensed someone kneel beside her. "You okay?"

Rachel looked over to see Jeanie. She felt ashamed that Jeanie would still talk with her after the picture she drew. "I sketched this garden in my room. I didn't know where I'd seen it, but obviously I saw it right here . . . This is the garden sketch Dani . . ." Rachel gritted her teeth. "I can't do this anymore. I'm so mad at her, Peter, Cayden . . . everyone! I just don't know what to do." She balled her hands into fists.

Jeanie tried to comfort her by patting her back. Rachel fought the tears that threatened to escape. What was it with Character Club and tears?

"I knew it was Mrs. Keller's garden the second I saw it. I didn't know you didn't know," Jeanie commented. "That's funny." Rachel smiled to see that Jeanie didn't seem angry with her.

Rachel took a good look at Jeanie. "I'm sorry. I should've forgiven you right away when you asked me to. And I shouldn't have drawn that horrible picture of you. I hope you will forgive me."

"Of course I will. I already did."

"You did?" Rachel questioned.

"Yeah. I've learned a lot about forgiveness since my dumb story got out." Jeanie sighed. She gave a little chuckle to try to lighten the mood.

"Yoo-hoo!" Mrs. Keller called.

The girls jumped. Rachel sniffed.

"Come on over to the yard, everyone. Make sure to take care of your garbage first."

Jeanie pulled a tissue out of her pocket and handed it to Rachel. "Sorry it's used, but it's better than a leaf."

Rachel laughed in spite of her distress and blew her nose on the wadded-up tissue. "Thanks for being a friend when I needed one."

Claire bounced over to them as they followed Mrs. Keller into the yard. Together they waited for the rest of the group.

Maggie came over with the other kids from the soccer game. Rachel could tell she noticed Rachel's splotchy face but quickly looked away. It felt like a knife in her back.

Mrs. Keller explained a game she called Yellow Card, Red Card. "You will all line up at the far end of the yard. I will stand at the other end holding up a yellow card, which means proceed with caution, or a red card, which means stop. If you don't stop . . ."

"You're out of the game!" Mr. Soccer, otherwise known as Ethan, interjected.

Mrs. Keller eyed Ethan but smiled. "Yes, but only if you don't freeze immediately."

"So is it kind of like Red Light, Green Light meets soccer referee?" Angel questioned with a giggle.

"You could say that," Mrs. Keller said with a smile. "Now go line up."

Rachel noticed Maggie follow Angel. The knife in Rachel's back turned. Rachel stood near Jeanie and Claire instead. All the students formed a ragged line at the far end of the yard.

"I will call out an action," Mrs. Keller

explained. "You will start toward me doing that action until the card changes color." She held up the yellow card and then said, "Hop."

Hopping across Mrs. Keller's yard proved to be a difficult task. Kids were knocking into each other, and it was easy to take one's eyes off Mrs. Keller. Rachel was grateful that she caught Mrs. Keller quietly switch to the red card. Rachel froze, but about half of the group did not.

Mrs. Keller asked them to sit along the side of the yard. Peter complained that she was too sneaky, as he skulked to the side. Ethan laughed and slapped him on the back as he walked with him. "Better luck next time, Pete."

When the group of kids who failed to freeze were off to the side, Mrs. Keller held up the yellow card again and said, "Spin."

Rachel groaned inwardly. She didn't like spinning. Jeanie and Claire took right off like little ballerinas. Rachel spun once and centered herself. She was about to spin again when she caught Maggie spinning right toward her giving her a nasty look. Their eyes locked. Rachel held a pained expression that turned Maggie's look into curiosity. Both girls missed Mrs. Keller hold up the red card. They spun toward Mrs. Keller right as she called them out.

Rachel followed Maggie to the side. Maggie squeezed into a small space between Angel and Wendy. Rachel had to go stand by Peter, who was still complaining about the unfairness of the game. Rachel watched with the loneliest feeling she'd ever had while the game played out. Even when her mom died, Maggie had been by her side.

Mrs. Keller switched back and forth between the cards until only Claire was left in the game. Mrs. Keller invited everyone back in for another round. She told them that she forgave them all for not paying better attention. Several kids chuckled at her comment but joined in for round two. They played three rounds before Mrs. Keller herded them all inside. She was ready to introduce the new virtue.

Once everyone settled on the floor, Mrs. Keller began, "Our virtue for this month is forgiveness. Forgiveness means to stop blaming or feeling anger toward someone who has hurt or wronged us."

Rachel's eyes widened. No wonder Mrs. Keller wanted her to come back. Rachel thought her face must be an easy book to read.

Rachel leaned back against the couch as Mrs. Keller's words sunk in. She hated the idea of letting Peter, Cayden, Jeanie, Dani, or even Maggie have any power over her. She looked down at her favorite white pair of jeans and replayed the worm incident in her mind again. She rubbed her finger over the faded but visible stain.

Mrs. Keller interrupted her thoughts when she changed the inflection of her voice. "Forgiveness has multiple layers and facets. It is simple but can also feel complicated. The first part to understanding forgiveness is to separate the action from the person. The action is something you can't undo. To replay the wrongdoing over and over again is only hurting you, not the person who did it to you."

Rachel's eyes shot up. She locked on Mrs. Keller's face. How did that woman always know what she was thinking?

Mrs. Keller kept talking. "Today we have a special guest with us to tell her story of forgiveness. It is a difficult story to listen to, but her life sets an example for us all. I'd like to introduce Miss Cornelia ten Boom." She waved her hand over the crowd and toward the kitchen.

In shuffled the small frame of Mrs. Keller's teenage daughter, Karlie, wearing glasses and a Dutch dress. She had her hair slicked back, powdered gray, and pulled into a bun. Karlie's older brother, Andrew, walked behind her wearing a German military uniform from the 1940s.

Karlie stood at the front of the room where her mother had just been. Andrew took a seat nearby. All the kids sat up a little straighter as it was always a treat when Karlie dressed in character. Plus, no one had ever seen Andrew dress up before!

Karlie began, "My name is Cornelia ten Boom. I was born on April 15, 1892. I was the third of four children. My family and friends called me Corrie. My father was a Dutch watchmaker. He was incredibly skilled, and I helped him in his shop that was attached to the front of our house.

"Besides helping him, my older sister, Betsie, and I ran a club for girls. Much like the one you all are attending, just without the boys." Karlie smiled as she looked out over the crowd. A few of the boys elbowed each other.

"But when I was forty-eight, the Nazis invaded our country. They banned our club and started relocating Jews. We didn't really know what this meant, but we knew it was wrong. Our neighbors were Jews. They were kind to everyone. They shouldn't have had to leave just because they were Jewish. We helped them however we could.

"Two years into the Nazi invasion, a woman came to us with a suitcase asking for help. She knew we had helped our neighbors. She was afraid to go home because Nazis had arrested her husband, and her son had gone into hiding. We invited her to move in with us until we could find a safe place for her. That was the beginning of our activity with the Dutch underground—a secret, illegal organization to help the Jews.

"We soon had many Jewish refugees coming to us for help. Food was scarce, so

Dutch people received ration cards to get weekly food coupons. Jewish people did not receive any.

"I remembered that an old friend worked in the local ration card office. I snuck to his house one evening planning to ask for five ration cards for our friends living with us. When he asked how many I needed, though, the number one hundred came out of my mouth! He staged a fake robbery at the office so he could get them for me. I distributed them to every Jew I met.

"Occasionally there would be raids by the Nazis, so we needed to have a place to hide the Jews living with us. A famous architect in Europe built a fake wall in my bedroom which created a hiding place. We held practice drills during which we would clear the kitchen of any trace of extra people eating there. We needed to get people into that small room in less than a minute. We installed a silent buzzer in the watch shop that rang back in the house. Anyone could start a drill by pushing the buzzer. Although our best efforts never made it in less than a minute, the practice provided something to do.

110

The challenge helped us escape the constant dread that surrounded our home. To keep us motivated, a sympathetic baker even provided cream puffs when we did well.

"Word of our work with the underground spread. The one hundred cards weren't nearly enough anymore. So many people with so many stories came through our watchmaker shop. The shop was headquarters to the operation.

"Then one fateful day in February I was raging with fever. An enemy disguised as someone who needed help came to me. I was too sick to catch that he wasn't acting right. He asked for money to release his wife from prison. I told him to come back in half an hour, closed the shop, and collapsed back into bed.

"I woke up to our warning buzzer going off and people scrambling through my room into the hiding place. I was completely confused at first but then woke up enough to realize this was a real raid. Soldiers stormed into my room, pulled me downstairs, asked me questions, and beat me. When I wouldn't talk, they beat my sister. Then they took everyone in our home off to jail. Everyone, that is, except the Jews they couldn't find hidden away.

"Jail was awful. I was separated from my father and sister. I was put in solitary confinement supposedly because I was sick. I spent my fifty-second birthday completely alone except for a few ants that frequented my cell."

Rachel knew what it felt like to be alone, but this was an unbearable kind of alone. She couldn't even imagine it.

Karlie continued as she touched her old, ragged costume, "I often worried about the Jews we left in the hiding place. Had they been found? Killed? Did someone rescue them? There was nothing else to do but think. I prayed for help to not worry and for their safety.

"In June all the women in the prison were moved to a concentration camp in Holland. I saw my sister after four months apart. We'd never been separated that long in our entire lives. We caught up on our difficult time apart during the train ride. Conditions were worse in our new prison, and we were forced to work long hours each day. We found reasons to hope, though. Betsie always found things to be thankful for. For me, it was such a relief to see and be with other people again.

"Three months later we took another train ride. We didn't know why and we didn't know where we were going. It was the most horrible ride of our lives. We were herded into a boxcar with no windows. Sixty women packed tight standing in one car where there was only room for thirty. We somehow all managed to sit down by wrapping our legs around each other and slowly squatting to a seated position. Getting back up was not an option.

"For four days we suffered in that train car with no food, no water, and no bathroom. We finally stopped on September 8, 1944. The train halted its miserable journey at Ravensbruck. The name struck fear in us all. It was a concentration camp near Berlin, Germany—the heart of the Nazi regime. This place was filled with horrors unimaginable. The guards mocked us and forced us naked into a shower room."

As Karlie explained this, Andrew, who had been quietly sitting to the side, rushed forward with a growl. Everyone jumped because he'd been so still they'd forgotten about him. He grabbed her arm roughly and yelled, "Clothes here on the floor! Then to the showers!" Andrew threw her down and glared with disdain. His sneer looked so evil. Rachel felt uncomfortable.

Karlie pulled herself up. She shuffled her feet and passed Andrew. He stormed out of the room.

Karlie continued, "After the humiliating showers, guards ushered us to barracks with square piers like bunk beds piled three high. There were no mattresses, though, only wood. Betsie and I were assigned a middle level. We had to share a square designed for four people with seven others—nine of us total. Turning over in the night was not a possibility. It was also crawling with fleas."

Rachel suddenly felt itchy. As she scratched her arm, she noticed several other kids doing the same.

"As the weather got colder, so did many

114

hearts," Karlie continued with a sad voice. "Betsie was always cheerful and continued to find things to be thankful for. Even as her health declined, women flocked to be around her. They would listen to her weak voice for hours.

"We passed time between work and painful hours standing at roll call by making plans of a home for people to come to when they were released. It would be a place to heal the emotional wounds of the war. We made plans to build window boxes and gardens in every color. Betsie's weakened body couldn't dampen her imagination. As she said herself, 'It will be so good for them . . . watching things grow. People can learn to love from flowers.'

"I enjoyed imagining and planning with her until I realized she planned to include Germans too. That was a bit too hard for me. They were the enemy. I would never forgive these awful people."

Rachel related. She didn't ever want to forgive her dad or Dani or . . . she had a list. It didn't matter how much she loved flowers. They can't teach you to love.

115

Karlie continued, "Sadly, Betsie's weakened body couldn't hold up against the abuse of this horrible prison. She died on December sixteenth at age fifty-nine."

Rachel sucked in her breath. This was supposed to be a happy-ending story. Not one filled with the death of people you love, like her own story.

"I, Cornelia ten Boom, was released nine days later on a 'clerical error.' It was a small miracle. I later found out that all the women my age were killed the very next week in the gas chambers."

Rachel shuddered. She had studied the gas chambers of the Holocaust before. Jews would think they were going in for a shower, but instead of water, poisonous gas rained down and killed everyone in the room.

Karlie kept telling Corrie's story. "It was a difficult journey home. I spent weeks in a hospital healing. But I was certainly free. My first question when I found my surviving family members was about the Jews we'd hidden during the raid. They told me that all the Jews in our hiding place were never found

116

by the Nazis. They survived. I was overjoyed and poured my energy into my new work. I followed Betsie's plan. I began rehabilitation centers for war victims.

"After about a year I began traveling the country. I shared my story and taught about forgiveness. I went all over Holland, parts of Europe, and even the United States. It was so difficult for me to go back to Germany. But Germany was where the people were most hungry for my story. Especially the soldiers who had been brainwashed by their officers to do the horrible things I experienced. It was the hardest place for me to speak.

"Then one night in Germany I had to face my worst fear. At the end of my talk, I saw one of the guards from Ravensbruck. He had been on guard at the showers. He was walking right toward me."

Andrew re-entered the room at that point. His face was warm and friendly like the Andrew Rachel was used to seeing. With a radiant smile, he held out his hand to Karlie. He said, "Thank you, Miss Corrie, for your message of forgiveness."

Karlie looked at his hand. Then she turned toward the kids sitting there with rapt attention. "I tried to smile and raise my hand." She swallowed and said, "I couldn't do it."

Rachel felt herself shaking her head with Corrie ten Boom. She wouldn't do it either if she was in her place.

Karlie bowed her head. "I felt nothing for this man, especially not forgiveness."

Andrew seemed oblivious to how long the two of them stood frozen there. Rachel was holding her breath. Her hands gripped her knees tightly.

Karlie persisted. "Somehow, though, after what felt like hours, my hand raised." Karlie paused. She ever so slowly brought her hand up to meet Andrew's. Rachel could feel herself struggling with Karlie to make the hand move. Rachel fought the movement while hoping for success at the same time.

"The moment I took his hand, a current seemed to pass between us. A love for this stranger overwhelmed me." Karlie took Andrew's hand. Their eyes met and they both smiled. Rachel felt a collective sigh in the room around her. She realized half of the kids had been holding their breath with her. She watched Karlie's body relax.

Karlie turned back to the kids and said, "Forgiving this enemy gave me a new kind of freedom."

Karlie and Andrew released their hands as she finished. The room was silent. The pair exited and Mrs. Keller took their place. She spoke softly, "I don't think I need to add anything else."

Rachel took a deep breath. She noticed Maggie across the room try to hide wiping a tear from her eye. Jeanie and Claire tightly gripped each other's hands. Glints of light reflected from the eyes of a few other girls. Even a few boys sat blinking hard.

Forgiveness seemed like very serious business. Rachel needed to get to work. Even if she didn't want to.

7 ~ Minefield

Rachel wasn't sure how to work on the business of forgiving. Maggie was still avoiding her, and it had been a long, lonely week. Maggie sat with Dani and Laura now. Dani had stopped texting Rachel altogether, but she could tell what Dani's daily texts said from watching her old group. Monday was now denim day. Tuesday they all wore black. Wednesday Rachel forced herself to stop noticing.

The only good thing that happened was the way Mrs. Potter twittered around the room each day in art class. She was proud of herself for convincing Robin Heller to be one of the judges for the art contest. Maybe Rachel would have a chance to meet her after all. If her dad would be around to remember to take her. It didn't look good. The show was this Saturday night.

On Thursday, Rachel put on her not-so-white jeans. They were turning into her Character Club uniform. Lucas offered to walk with her after school. Rachel couldn't tell if he noticed that she and Maggie weren't talking. It felt good to be with someone, though.

When they arrived at Mrs. Keller's home, Andrew and Karlie were handing out rocks in various sizes. Andrew handed Rachel a pear-sized rock and gave her a wink. He handed Lucas an orange-sized one with a slap on his back.

Mrs. Keller explained, "Today you need to hold on to these rocks for every activity we do. You cannot put them down for any reason. If you need to use the restroom, they go with you."

A bunch of the boys chuckled. Peter

tried to toss his softball-sized rock up like it weighed nothing. He almost dropped it as the weight pulled his arms down when he caught it.

"We will do a popular activity called minefield. The yard will be littered with make-believe land mines. It would be extremely dangerous to step on any of them."

"Can we pretend to blow up if we step on one?" Cayden called out. A few boys laughed.

"Sure," Mrs. Keller answered. "But anyone who doesn't make it to the other side safely is considered dead. If you are dead, you can't participate in the rest of the day's activities."

Cayden quieted at that. No one ever knew what Mrs. Keller had up her sleeve. It wasn't worth messing around if it meant missing one of her surprises. He cradled his grapefruit-sized rock in both hands.

"Now, let's create some obstacles." Mrs. Keller picked up a piece of paper. "What are some of the things people might do to hurt you, physically or emotionally or in any other way?"

Rachel wondered where to start. She sure had a list.

Amanda—standing between Valerie and Maria—made a comment. "My older sister stole my favorite shirt yesterday and won't give it back."

"Okay." Mrs. Keller wadded the piece of paper up in a ball and threw it into the yard. "That's one land mine. Amanda, would you like to wad one up too, since it was your suggestion?"

Mrs. Keller held out a piece of paper to her. Amanda took it and tried to wad it up with one hand since her rock was in the other. She did her best and tossed it into the yard. Valerie and Maria consoled her. Rachel sensed the overdramatization.

Ethan spoke next. "My little sister keeps stealing my soccer ball."

"Thanks, Ethan." Mrs. Keller smiled as she held out a piece of paper to him. He crumpled it by smashing it against his rock. Ethan threw it a few feet away from Amanda's.

"Destroying other people's property,"

Maggie called out as she cast a nasty glance at Rachel.

Rachel sucked in her breath. Maggie was so clueless.

Valerie offered, "Someone posted a lie about something that happened at my birthday party on social media. It was really rude." She glanced apologetically at Rachel.

Other kids continued to share. Rachel's heart began to beat faster. So many bad things kept happening to her that she didn't even know which one to choose. She wanted to say something, but what?

It was nice of Valerie to say the first thing Dani did to her so she didn't have to. However, there was so much more. She noticed Maggie's head had cocked funny when Valerie shared. Maybe she was starting to put two and two together.

Rachel's palms began to sweat as she watched student after student wad up their pieces of paper and throw them into the yard. The rock became wet in her hand.

The grass became littered with paper clumps. Rachel wondered how anyone could cross without stepping on something. As much as she wanted to share, she didn't want to "blow up" either.

Finally the group started to run out of ideas, and Mrs. Keller held up one last piece of paper. "Anyone just burning up inside wanting to share one last thing?" Her eyes actually met Rachel's.

Rachel felt sick to her stomach, but she couldn't keep it in any longer. She blurted out, "The garden picture in the office was mine!" Everyone turned to look at her. She continued bravely, "Dani stole my phone and claimed that she drew that picture."

The group quieted. Rachel looked at Maggie. Maggie's eyes widened in realization as Rachel took the last piece of paper and wadded it up. She hurled it onto the lawn with the others.

Mrs. Keller broke the awkward silence by saying, "Thank you, Rachel. I'm glad you got that burden off your chest."

Mrs. Keller instructed the students, "Partner up. One of you will be blindfolded as the other one tries to lead you through the minefield. You will need to trust your partner to make it across the yard safely without stepping on any of these obstacles. Go ahead."

Maggie raced toward Rachel. "How could I have been so dumb! I'm so sorry! Can you ever forgive me?"

Rachel looked at Maggie and was flooded with relief. She knew she didn't need to think about it or wait for another time. She felt like Corrie ten Boom as she said, "Of course."

It amazed Rachel at how easy it was to forgive Maggie. Maggie bear-hugged her best friend. Rachel was overcome with a sense of gratitude. The last week of loneliness vanished in an instant. Rachel and Maggie grabbed hands as the others partnered up.

Mrs. Keller continued, "Go ahead and choose which one of you will lead and which one of you gets the blindfold."

Rachel agreed to be blindfolded. She wanted to block out everything but Maggie's wonderful voice talking to her again.

Andrew and Karlie handed out a different-colored scarf to each pair of partners. Rachel tied hers around her head covering her eyes. She actually did feel a little bit lighter, even though it made Dani a public enemy. Maggie was back—sweet, reliable Maggie.

Maggie led her to the edge of the minefield. They both clutched their heavy rocks in their hands.

When the others had gathered, Mrs. Keller reminded them of the rules. She told the seeing partner to begin leading the blindfolded partner through the obstacles and across the lawn to safety.

Maggie wasn't allowed to touch Rachel but could speak directions to her. Rachel felt frustrated. It seemed like every time she took a step, Maggie told her to stop or freeze or turn right or left. Rachel focused and obeyed.

After what felt like far too long, Maggie let out a squeal and Rachel felt herself wrapped in another big hug. Maggie pulled the blindfold off to reveal they were safely across the lawn. Ethan and Lucas, plus a few other groups, had made it as well. Peter and Cayden were not even halfway across.

Peter was blindfolded but kept arguing with Cayden no matter what Cayden told him to do. He shuffled his feet along. Rachel expected him to step on a mine at any moment.

Jeanie and Claire finished a few moments after Maggie and Rachel. The pairs high-fived each other and then cheered on the other teams. Amazingly, Peter and Cayden made it across but not without yelling at each other quite a bit.

Mrs. Keller asked a few volunteers to collect all the papers in a big basket. She then led the group into her living room and sat them all down on the floor. "Let's debrief, ladies and gentlemen. First of all, congratulations! We didn't lose a single pair during that exercise. What were your feelings as you participated in that activity?"

"I thought it was hard to trust Claire to guide me even though she's my best friend," Jeanie explained. "I'm glad I did, though, because we made it." Jeanie gave Claire a big smile.

Peter complained, "It would have been easier if Cayden could give directions."

"Well, it would have been easier if you could listen!" Cayden whined back. He gave

Peter a shove.

Mrs. Keller interrupted, "Okay, boys. It was designed to be a challenging task. Every day in our lives we come across obstacles. With each one, we have a choice. We can let that obstacle ruin us or . . ." She paused to pull out one of the papers from the basket. She carefully opened up the wad and flattened it out on the floor in front of her. She smoothed it over as best she could with her hands. "Or we can choose to forgive."

She held up the wrinkled paper. "If you look at this paper, you will notice it is not perfect anymore. When I choose to forgive someone for the wrong they have done to me, the offense is no longer a dangerous land mine that can destroy me. That doesn't mean that I don't have scars. There are still wrinkles in this paper. But the power of the person who hurt me is broken. It no longer strangles and threatens to destroy me. I can move on. I stop giving the offender the power to keep hurting me."

Mrs. Keller continued, "In your hands you should still be holding a heavy rock. Today it has represented a burden you carry. The burden is a grudge. When we choose to withhold forgiveness, it becomes this heavy thing we carry everywhere we go. If you remember Corrie ten Boom's story from last week, her hardship was lifting her hand in forgiveness to shake that German soldier's hand. When she forgave him, it was like dropping her rock. No matter how long you've been angry, it's time to let go."

She paused to make eye contact with several kids around the room. Rachel looked down at her rock.

"It's time to forgive," Mrs. Keller said. "The only person you hurt when you don't forgive is yourself. The person who hurt you isn't carrying the rock. You are. If you want to choose to forgive someone you've been holding a grudge against, take your rock outside to my garden. Burdens are no longer heavy when you lay them down."

Amanda immediately stood and said, "I'm going to forgive my sister for taking my shirt. It's really nothing compared to what Corrie forgave." She walked out the door with her rock.

Ethan stood next and announced, "Maybe if I just play soccer more with my little sister, Harley, she won't want to steal my ball anymore. I'm gonna forgive her." He followed Amanda out the door.

Peter stood up and headed for the garden. He called back over his shoulder, "Cayden, I forgive you for being terrible at giving directions!" A few kids chuckled. Rachel could see Amanda, Ethan, and Peter piling their rocks in the garden. She could see it adding to the beauty of Mrs. Keller's creative placement of her flowers. One by one, more kids left the room and began placing their rocks in the garden. Some of them made comments as they left the room. Others walked out silently.

Maggie elbowed Rachel and then gave a nod that they should head outside. Rachel stood with Maggie. They walked out together, but Rachel hid her rock behind her back when Maggie laid hers down.

As the kids mingled in the backyard, Andrew and Karlie occasionally poked their heads out the door. They would call a name of someone whose parents were there to pick them up. Maggie's name was one of them. She gave Rachel a hug and said she'd see her on Monday. Friday was a teacher in-service day, so there wouldn't be any school.

Rachel stood by the garden with her rock still behind her back. Valerie came over to Rachel and told her, "I knew Dani didn't draw that sketch. I saw it on your phone when you left it at my party. Dani took your phone and said she would give it back to you. I had no idea what she was planning. I'm really sorry too."

Rachel gave Valerie a weak smile. "Thanks. She sure has changed over the last few weeks."

"Yeah. I don't think I'll be inviting her to any more parties. And I'm going to tell Mr. Bostrick that she stole your picture."

Rachel opened her mouth to argue, but Karlie called out Valerie's name. Valerie gave Rachel a little squeeze and ran in through the house.

Rachel was emotionally exhausted. She couldn't bring herself to walk away from Mrs. Keller's garden even after most of the kids had left.

Rachel settled herself down on one of Mrs. Keller's red outdoor couches. She made sure not to sit on the one she'd been sitting on when the boys threw the worms on her. Besides, this one had a better view of the garden.

She stared at all the rocks the other kids had added to the garden. Then she looked at her own rock that she held in her lap. It seemed that someone would get away with something awful if she put it down. She didn't know who it would be. Peter? Dani? Her dad?

Rachel leaned her head back on the cushion. She looked up through the wooden pergola that covered the patio. There was a small overhang from the house that protected the couches from the elements. A tree rose from behind the garden. Its branches reached out, covering part of the pergola, providing some extra shelter. The wind was picking up, causing the tree above her to sway.

Rachel sat mesmerized by the motion of the leaves and the branches. Maybe a storm was brewing. There was definitely one building within her. The rock, clenched in her hand, was a constant reminder. She felt her eyelids getting heavy. The breeze lulled her into unconsciousness.

Rachel awoke to a gentle hand on her shoulder. She opened her eyes to see Mrs. Keller sitting beside her on the couch. "Rough day, dear one?" Mrs. Keller's eyes smiled as big as her heart.

Rachel looked around to see if anyone else was still there. She nodded slowly.

"They're all gone," Mrs. Keller comforted.

Rachel looked out beyond Mrs. Keller to where the backyard ended and the big sky began. She could see the mountains out to the west and the sun beginning to set behind them. How long had she slept?

A localized thunderstorm was brewing a bit to the north. The oranges, pinks, and purples of those clouds were gorgeous. The rumbling thunder unnerved her a little, though.

Mrs. Keller continued, "I don't know this girl Dani . . . and what she did was extremely unkind. But I don't think it's worth holding so tightly to that rock of yours."

Looking from the rock to Mrs. Keller, Rachel started, "It's not just that. I really should have five rocks. I'm mad at so many people right now."

"I see." Mrs. Keller nodded and thought for a minute. Then she stood and walked past her garden to her xeriscaped area. She stooped and picked up several white rocks. They were part of a larger arrangement made to look like a small stream pouring out of a larger rock. She walked back and sat by Rachel again. "Let's trade that one hefty rock for several smaller ones. You can take as many as you need."

Rachel handed Mrs. Keller her big rock and took two smaller white ones. "These are for Peter and Cayden. I never really forgave them for dumping those worms on me. I still have a stain on my favorite jeans." She rubbed a finger over her pants. "But it does seem stupid to stay mad after all the stuff Corrie ten Boom chose to forgive."

Rachel pulled herself to stand. She placed the two small stones on the pile of bigger ones where the others had placed theirs earlier. She came back and sat by Mrs. Keller. Rachel took another white rock from her and turned it around in her fingers. "This one should be for Dani. I want to hate her. I want her to be miserable. I don't really want to let it go."

"But do you see how she's not the one hurting when you hold on to the anger? By not forgiving her, you let her keep hurting you."

"I guess so. But I'm just so angry."

"I want to show you something." Mrs. Keller stood and walked around the side of the house.

Rachel stood again with the small rock in her hand. She followed Mrs. Keller to the front yard by the flag pole where Rachel had pulled the weeds last week. She couldn't believe her eyes when she looked down. It didn't look like she had done a thing! All the little leaf sprouts were back.

"Your anger is a symptom of something much bigger. Unforgiveness is like a weed, Rachel. If you don't get down and pull it by the root, it comes right back. You need to yank all the anger out and get rid of every bit of it or it keeps haunting you, turning you bitter like a bad herb. I watched you last week. Your effort was halfhearted. Just like your acceptance of Peter and Cayden's apology. I think you got to the root of that today.

"You thought you were helping last week when you pulled these weeds for me. But if you just break off the stem, the roots down below continue feeding the weed, allowing it to grow again. Forgiveness is the same. Do you want to allow Dani to hurt you over and over again?"

"No. No I don't."

"That's good. Let's go back and get rid of her rock."

"Can I pull some of these weeds the right way first?" Rachel asked.

"Of course!" Mrs. Keller disappeared for a moment to grab her shovel. The thunder rumbled in the distance.

When she returned, she demonstrated the proper weed-plucking action again.

Rachel watched closely and realized what she had missed last week. She took the shovel and made sure she pulled the root up with the stems this time. It was a little awkward with Dani's rock still in one hand, but she persevered. Mrs. Keller nodded in approval.

After Rachel cleared the area a second time, she stood to survey her work. "It looks like it did last week now."

"Yes, but this time, I know you got the roots." The duo headed around the house to the backyard. They stopped at the pile of rocks.

Rachel looked at the pile and then at the small rock in her hand. Instead of adding it to the others, she wound up and hurled it as far as she could. It went over Mrs. Keller's back fence and into the open space behind.

"Impressive!" Mrs. Keller encouraged. "Do you need any more?" She held her hands open in front of Rachel. There were two more small stones.

Rachel knew who they were for. She sank down beside Mrs. Keller. She took the last two stones. "Those are for my mom and dad."

Rachel looked up into Mrs. Keller's eyes, which were filled with concern. Rachel's heart beat faster. "My mom died last year. Why did she leave me? My dad won't talk about her. He hasn't paid any attention to me since the accident. I even had a chance to meet my favorite artist last week and he completely forgot. He didn't even care when I told him!" Rachel's pent-up tears flowed at last.

"Oh, my dear child." Mrs. Keller embraced Rachel while she cried. The storm overhead released its torrents as well. The pounding rain drowned out the sound of Rachel's wails as it pounded the roof above them. Rachel's grip relaxed around the last two stones, and they dropped to the patio as Mrs. Keller continued to hold her.

Rachel wept for a long time but eventually ran out of tears as the storm died down. Karlie appeared in the doorway announcing she had made dinner.

Mrs. Keller helped Rachel up and said, "Let's get you some nourishment. Then I'll text your dad and let him know you're spending the night with us. I have a trick that may fix those jeans. I also have a special place I want to take you tomorrow since you don't have school."

8 ~ Botanicals

Karlie's dinner was amazing. Rachel wondered how a girl only a few years older had become such a good cook. As she shoveled the delicious potatoes, meat, and salad into her mouth, she enjoyed listening to the three Kellers banter back and forth. They seemed to get along so well and really enjoy being together.

All three asked Rachel questions to make her feel welcome as well. It felt completely surreal to be sitting at Mrs. Keller's dinner table with her family and planning to spend the night. Rachel kept pinching herself to check that it wasn't a dream.

After dinner, Karlie gave Rachel one of her nightshirts to sleep in. Rachel changed into it and met Mrs. Keller in the laundry room. Mrs. Keller grabbed some bleach and spot-treated Rachel's jeans. Rachel watched carefully but let Mrs. Keller do the work. Then she decided to ask the question she'd been wondering for weeks. "Mrs. Keller, is there a Mr. Keller?"

Mrs. Keller set the pants on the edge of the washing machine and turned to Rachel. "Yes." She paused and added in a whisper, "I believe there is."

Rachel creased her eyebrows in confusion.

Mrs. Keller clarified, "He is in the US Air Force. About two years ago, his plane disappeared. He is considered MIA, or Missing in Action. We've been told to give up hope, but I refuse to."

Rachel couldn't decide if that was smart or not. But then, if there was a chance she could see her mother again, she'd like to believe it was possible. The hope of it all seemed like a good idea.

"Okay," Mrs. Keller announced, "You go on and get some sleep and I'll see what I can do about this." She led Rachel to the guest room where Rachel collapsed for the night. She slept better than she had in weeks.

The next morning, her jeans were outside the guest room door. Rachel picked them up to inspect them. She was amazed that she couldn't even tell which leg the stain had been removed from! She pulled them on. Rachel raced downstairs to thank Mrs. Keller.

After a delicious breakfast, Mrs. Keller announced that she was taking them to the botanical gardens. Karlie gasped in delight. Andrew smiled a casual smile. Rachel asked, "What are bi-onical gardens?"

Karlie laughed out loud. "It's bo-tan-i-cal gardens. And it is the most beautiful place in the city!"

When Mrs. Keller, Andrew, Karlie, and Rachel arrived at the gardens, Rachel's eyes widened at the beauty all around her. For the first time in her life she saw plants like blue delphinium, orange dahlias, and pink echinacea. She knew their names because they were each labeled. The mixture of colors danced before her eyes. The scents delighted her nostrils.

At one point she breathed in a scent that took her back many years. She was sitting in the bathroom watching her mom get ready for a date. Rachel hugged her knees while trying to stay balanced on the closed toilet lid.

"Why d'you haf to get ready to go out wif Daddy?" five-year-old Rachel asked. Her mom glanced at her sideways and grinned. She picked up a bottle of plumeria perfume. She squirted it on her wrist and rubbed it against her other wrist. Then she squirted Rachel's little ball of a body. Rachel sniffed deeply. "We smell like fowers, Momma."

"Yes, and Daddy loves us that way!"

"Then you should wear this efery day," Rachel suggested.

"I guess I should." Rachel's mom chased her from the bathroom trying to tickle her.

Rachel flinched as if her mother had poked her in the side. Her mom had worn that perfume every day after that until . . .

Rachel looked up and saw a small plumeria tree above her. Once she put her nose to it, her heart ached with sadness. It smelled just like her mother used to smell. Since the car accident, she'd completely forgotten about it.

After exploring the various gardens, the foursome sat down to enjoy the packed lunch Mrs. Keller had prepared. They sat on a luscious lawn overlooking the lily pad ponds.

Several small children squatted along the edge looking for frogs. Two brothers about three years old pointed at all the different kinds of water bugs. Their mom sat by a double stroller on a shaded bench a few yards behind them texting on her phone.

A few college-age guys came by with fancy cameras. They paused to snap some photos of the more impressive-looking flowers. A few little old ladies had easels set up; they were painting their own versions of the water lilies.

Six teenagers took turns snapping pictures of the rest of their group acting like a totem pole in front of the beautiful scene.

Then they raced to see who could post it to social media first.

Rachel heard the two little boys getting excited. "Look! A froggie!" one exclaimed. He leaned farther over the edge of the pond as he pointed. He lost his balance and grabbed his brother to steady himself. It didn't help and they both plunged into the shallow pool.

Karlie raced over and pulled one out of the water before the mother even put her phone down. He cried and ran to his mother as Karlie rescued the other shocked boy.

The first boy angrily kicked his mom and yelled, "You made me fall. Now I all wet. Bad Mommy!"

Shocked, Rachel observed the mother, who snapped right back, "I did not! I'm way over here."

Karlie stood between the two boys. The second one she pulled out was still clinging to her as he dripped on the pavement. "What I saw happen," Karlie started in a voice that urged an audience, "was two curious little boys leaning over the water's edge. I saw one spy something dart away from him. What was it?"

"A baby froggie," answered the boy who was still clinging to her. The other boy took a step away from his mother and closer to Karlie.

Karlie continued, "Then one of those curious boys leaned waaay out to get a closer look, and then what happened?"

"I fell in!" the boy standing by Karlie offered.

"Yes," Karlie agreed. "You lost your balance, grabbed your brother, and then what happened?"

"I fell too!" the other boy added, stepping in reach of Karlie.

Karlie finished, "You both tumbled in!" She rolled her hands over each other and then threw them in the air acting like she had just told the funniest story. "Do you guys remember that?"

The boys nodded and started to smile. "And now look at you both! You are all wet and cool on a hot, sunny day!" She finished with a flair, holding her arms over her stomach and belly-laughing. The boys started giggling with her.

The mom stood and joined them. Her

eyes shone, and she mouthed, "Thank you." Then she took each boy by the hand and ushered them to the stroller.

Karlie came back and joined the trio still enjoying their picnic.

"How'd you do that?" Rachel asked in shock.

"Sometimes when you are surprised or hurt by something, your brain panics. But if you can move the event into the logical part of your brain by explaining or talking through the event, it calms your brain down. I learned that from Mom."

Mrs. Keller smiled. "The amygdala is the part of your brain that causes it to fight, flight, or freeze. You want to get your brain to use the prefrontal cortex, which holds the logic part of your brain. It's a good exercise to try when you worry too much."

"That's a lot of really big words," Rachel said as she pondered the new information.

"It also protects the heart from becoming hardened," Mrs. Keller continued. "That boy instantly got angry with his mother. Karlie dismantled that with distraction. He will remember that event as something funny that happened to him, not something he blamed his mother for."

"I wish I could have done that before I destroyed Dani's print of my sketch. It did look nice in that frame. I just couldn't stand to see her name on my picture."

"Remember the weeds. The longer you wait to deal with something, the deeper it grows and the harder it is to pull out. In today's case, we yanked them out before they ever took root. There's a lot of people who let those roots grow deep. They get thicker and wilder the deeper they go."

"People like me?"

"Only you can answer that, Rachel. It only takes one person to forgive. It takes two people to restore a relationship. Some relationships you need to just let go. Others are worth the risk to try to save."

"I don't think I want to restore a friendship with Dani, but I do need my dad, don't I?"

Mrs. Keller leaned her forehead into Rachel's and said, "I would think so."

The group of four gathered up their picnic leftovers. Rachel left the Kellers to throw away her trash. When she lifted the lid to the trash can, she looked through a group of rosebushes and sucked in her breath. Rachel saw Dani walking down the path with Brian! Rachel ducked behind a tree to watch. She couldn't quite pinpoint her feelings. Seeing Dani bubbled up some of the old anger, but she tried to believe that she had forgiven her.

Brian headed toward the new science center, but Dani kept grabbing his arm and showing him different flowers. She was wearing a pale yellow sundress and sandals that would have blistered Rachel's heels. Rachel stifled her gag reflex. She watched Dani try to pick a rose. A thorn stabbed her finger. "Oh, Brian! My finger!" she cried with a flair.

Rachel rolled her eyes as the drama unfolded. Brian didn't look too sympathetic. Dani squeezed her finger to show that she was indeed bleeding. It was quite a production.

Brian shrugged and said, "Let's see if there's a napkin in the snack shop."

The two started walking toward Rachel.

Rachel ducked down to hide. She saw a rock on the ground that looked eerily familiar to the rock representing her grudge against Dani. Was that just yesterday she hurled that over Mrs. Keller's fence? Rachel's fingers closed around it. She stood and turned. Mrs. Keller stood right behind her offering a Band-Aid. The look in Mrs. Keller's eyes said, "The choice is yours."

Rachel tightened her grip on the rock, then accepted the Band-Aid. "Thanks," she muttered.

Rachel rounded the rosebush and held the two items behind her back. She stopped a few feet in front of the couple. She gripped the rock tighter. She wanted to throw it at Dani. Then she again remembered hurtling Dani's rock over Mrs. Keller's fence last night. Her grip loosened. Slowly she lifted her hand holding the Band-Aid. She looked at it and then up at Dani. "Hey, Dani. I see you cut yourself on a rose thorn."

A look of surprise developed in both Dani's and Brian's faces. Dani's included a hint of fear. Brian's looked amused. Rachel continued before she lost her nerve, "I just happen to have a Band-Aid. Here you go." Rachel held it out to Dani.

The shock on Dani's face could not be hidden. Dani opened her mouth but nothing came out. Brian's grin grew bigger. "Hey, thanks! That was super nice of you." He turned to Dani and said, "Wasn't it, Dani?"

Dani just nodded slowly. Brian tapped her chin to remind her to close her mouth. He turned to Rachel and said, "I was just telling Dani about what a good artist you are." He reached for the Band-Aid.

Dani snapped out of her stupor. She shook Brian off.

"I believe she's seen my art." Rachel grimaced. Her hand tightened around the rock. She pictured the little boy kicking at his mom. The memory of Jeanie offering forgiveness flashed across Rachel's mind. She saw Karlie taking Andrew's hand as they dressed in their World War II garb. Rachel loosened her grip on the rock and released it. The rock fell with a thud to the ground and bounced away.

Rachel set her shoulders straight and smiled her best forgiving smile. "I forgive you, Dani." She felt a release inside her. It felt like she'd just dropped a ten-ton boulder. She teased, "Better get that finger bandaged. Wouldn't want it to bleed on that lovely dress."

Rachel spun before she said anything else. She made her way back around the roses. Mrs. Keller waited on the other side and gave her a big hug. "So that was your dear old Dani?"

Rachel just nodded. They caught up with Andrew and Karlie and headed the opposite direction of Dani and Brian.

It wasn't long before they came upon a large pile of stones. Mrs. Keller pointed it out and asked, "Rachel, do you know what that's called?"

"A rock garden?" Rachel guessed.

"Well, yes." Mrs. Keller chuckled. "It's also called a cairn. In sixteenth-century Scotland people built cairns to commemorate an event or remember a special person. I want you to take a good look at that cairn, Rachel. It can commemorate the day you chose to forgive. It is something you can look back upon and tell yourself, 'I forgave that incident. It has no power over me anymore.'"

"Hold on." Rachel turned and ran back to the spot where she had confronted Dani. Her eyes scanned the ground for that unique rock. It was there by the edge of the path resting in the mulch. Rachel grabbed it and ran back to Mrs. Keller. She knelt down and looked at her rock. She balanced it on top of the cairn and said, "I choose to forgive." Rachel stood up and looked at her addition to the cairn. She snapped a picture of it with her phone to help her remember.

Mrs. Keller put her arm around Rachel and smiled. They meandered through the other sections of beautiful gardens. Mrs. Keller taught Rachel the names of the different flowers and even some of their meanings.

"Is there a flower that means forgiveness?" Rachel asked.

"Actually there are several flowers that represent forgiveness. They seem to be spring bulbs, though, so we can't find them this time of year. Purple hyacinths can mean 'I'm sorry' or 'please forgive me.' And I read once that giving someone white tulips tells them that you wish for them to forgive you and that you want a fresh start. Daffodils can also be used to tell someone you want to put the past behind you and begin a new season of happiness."

"I don't know what a hyacinth or daffodil looks like, but I do know tulips. Maybe I'll draw one for my dad."

The group decided to relax in the songbird garden. There were several benches and bird feeders positioned around the shaded area. Mrs. Keller explained that her family enjoys taking a few minutes to be quiet in this specific garden to listen to the beautiful birdcalls. The four of them spread out in various locations.

Andrew sat on a stump and started reading something on his phone. Karlie perched herself on a bench and pulled a book out of her little cinch sack. Mrs. Keller sat perfectly straight on a bench and closed her eyes.

Rachel could hear the different birdcalls but knew her heart was too restless just to sit there. She pulled her sketchbook out of her backpack. She closed her eyes to try to picture white tulips. Once she could see them in her mind, she opened her eyes to re-create them on paper.

As Rachel finished her tulip bouquet, a beautiful songbird came and perched on a branch just beyond her reach. Rachel sucked in her breath trying not to scare it away. Her pencil started flying over the page in an attempt to re-create the tiny bird's form on her paper. His little head turned toward her as if he had planned to pose for his portrait all along.

Rachel enjoyed seeing the sketch take shape. She kept glancing back to make sure her model was still there. Rachel smiled as she finished her sketch. She carefully held it up to show him. The bird nodded as if he approved and flew off.

Rachel looked up and all three Kellers were staring at her. Andrew and Karlie jumped up and ran over.

"That was amazing!" Karlie squealed. "Can I see your sketch?"

Rachel proudly showed them the picture of her tiny model. She could tell they were impressed.

Mrs. Keller beamed. She joined them and shared, "Encounters with nature are very special gifts. Keep this close to your heart."

Rachel smiled and hugged her sketchbook. Maybe she had room in her heart to forgive her dad after all. "I'd like to show this to my dad. I think I'm ready to go talk with him. I want to forgive him, too, and try to restore our relationship."

Mrs. Keller smiled and nodded. "Let's get you home."

9 ~ Homecoming

Rachel walked in the door and dropped her backpack on the floor. This time she felt hopeful for a new beginning. The weight she had carried around for the last month had lifted. She couldn't wait to show her sketch to her dad.

"Dad!" she called. There was no answer. "Dad!" she called again as she wandered the house. Rachel frowned as she realized her dad wasn't home. Why would he be? It was only three o'clock on a Friday afternoon. Tomorrow night was the art show. Why did she think anything would change?

Rachel crossed the room to head upstairs. She caught sight of her art supply cabinet. The pencils still lay under her dad's desk where they had rolled so many weeks ago. Rachel decided to turn a new leaf. She would clean up her mess. She crawled under the desk to retrieve the pencils and found an envelope by them. It must have fallen behind her dad's desk. The date of Robin Heller's art class was written on it. Plus the words DON'T FORGET.

Rachel picked up the pencils and envelope. She tried to turn on the desk light, but it didn't turn on. The envelope was torn open. Rachel pulled out the papers inside. There were three of them. The first was a hospital bill that said FINAL NOTICE. Rachel had never thought that her dad would still need to be paying for her mom's time in the hospital.

The second was an electric bill that said OVERDUE. Rachel went to the kitchen and tried to turn on the light. That one was out too. Had the electric company shut off their power?

The last was the flyer for the art class. Rachel caught her breath when she saw the fee. How had she missed that before? There was no way her dad could afford to take her with all these other problems.

Rachel ran her finger over the date. She stood up and set the papers on her dad's desk. That settled it. There would be no art show tomorrow night. Rachel decided that it wasn't her dad's fault. If she was going to forgive and restore, she'd have to let go of some things. Even hard things. Rachel carried her pencils upstairs to her room. She sighed as she flopped down on her bed. How long would she need to wait before her father came home? How could she help him when he did?

Rachel opened her sketchbook to the tulip page. She picked up a yellow pencil and started to color the bird's feathers. Then she remembered the flowers in her parents' old room. She wandered down the hall. The curtains were pulled and the light wouldn't turn on. She tried to see the flower on the old

159

shelf above the cabinet. She squinted for a better look. It appeared to be a tulip. It was a dusty tan. Rachel guessed it was once white. She realized that the empty vial of her mother's plumeria perfume was holding the flower. It was like her mom was asking for forgiveness from beyond. Rachel wondered if the bottle still held the scent of her mother's perfume. She wanted to smell it again.

Rachel opened the cabinet. She removed the books from the bottom three cubbies on the right side below the shelf. Empty, she could use them like a ladder to climb up to reach the flower. Rachel grabbed on to an upper shelf and put her foot in the bottom cubicle. She gasped as she felt the cabinet wobble a bit. It seemed so strong and sturdy. After all, it was over two hundred years old. It should be built to last.

She placed her other foot on the next shelf up. She was off the ground but couldn't quite reach the flower on the shelf above the cabinet yet. One more step should do it. She focused on her balance.

Rachel took her bottom foot and

moved it up toward the third shelf. Before she reached it, she felt the cabinet tilt toward her. She tried to jump off and push it back toward the wall, but the momentum of all the items on the shelves was too much. Books, knickknacks, and breakables came tumbling toward her. There was no time to jump out of the way. The sound of glass breaking and books pounding the floor deafened her. The falling items knocked her to the floor.

It felt as if time went into slow motion. Rachel stared up in horror. The cabinet was coming down too. She tried to scramble out of the way. She wasn't quick enough.

Rachel screamed as she watched the cabinet coming toward her. Right before she felt she was about to take her last breath, the cabinet shuddered to a stop. The top part of the cabinet had landed on the bed and pinned her to the floor. As she tried to assess if she was hurt or not, she heard feet pounding up the stairs.

"Rachel! Rachel, what was that? Are you okay?" Her dad was yelling as he bolted through the house toward the noise.

"Dad!" Rachel called out.

Rachel saw her dad burst through the door. "What!? How?! Are you okay?"

Rachel answered, "I think so. I'm just stuck."

Her dad threw the curtains open to let the sunlight into the room so he could see her. "Give me your arms." Her dad reached out for both of her hands.

Rachel held them out for her dad to grab. He pulled slowly, and she felt herself moving.

"It's working. I'm not as stuck as I thought."

Rachel's dad pulled her carefully out from all the rubble. Before she could say anything, her dad collapsed beside her and grabbed her in the tightest hug she'd ever felt.

Rachel released another flood of emotion she'd been holding back. It seemed that since the dam broke with Mrs. Keller, the river just kept flowing. "I was so scared," Rachel mumbled into her dad's shirt, tears freely flowing.

"I was scared too. That thing weighs a

ton. I've already lost your mother. I can't lose you too. Are you hurt?" He choked back a sob as he checked her over.

Rachel shook her head and clung to him for the first time since her mother's funeral. He released a flood of emotion she hadn't seen since the night at the hospital. Maybe his dam was breaking too. They held each other for a long time.

"I'm so sorry, Dad. I just wrecked our antique."

Rachel's dad disagreed. "I doubt it. These things are beasts. Thank goodness the bed was there to block the fall. You'd have been crushed. How did it happen?"

Rachel's tears turned solemn. "I was climbing up to get Mom's perfume bottle. I smelled her today at the gardens."

"Oh." He stood up and easily reached the shelf that held the small treasure. He removed it and paused to look at the flower for a moment. He pulled Rachel up, and they sat on the unburied half of the bed together.

Rachel took it from him. She pulled out the tulip and sniffed the vial. She wasn't sure if she imagined the plumeria or really smelled it. Either way, it felt like her mother was sitting there with them.

Rachel handed the flower to her dad and explained, "It's a tulip. Mrs. Keller said that giving someone a white tulip tells them that you want them to forgive you. I felt like Mom was asking me to forgive her for dying."

Rachel's dad sat silently beside her looking at the flower. Finally he said, "I guess this year has been pretty hard on us both. I was too busy grieving to think about how you were handling it. I figured you had all your friends to talk to."

He looked at Rachel, and Rachel saw another tear fall down his cheek. "I want to talk about her with you, Dad."

"I'm sorry I haven't been able to talk much. I'm sorry that I wasn't here sooner. I'm sorry we have no electricity. I'm sorry for a lot of things." Rachel's dad took her face in his hands and looked her in the eye. "I'm so sorry, Rachel. Can you forgive me?"

Rachel never expected to hear her dad apologize for anything. She nodded her head with new energy through happy tears.

"Oh, thank you, sweet girl of mine. I've had my priorities all messed up lately. I thought if I worked more and got the bills paid, that would be enough. But I haven't been strong for you or even here for you. But that doesn't mean I don't care about you."

Rachel beamed. Her dad's eyes continued to glisten. She realized she didn't know what was going on in her dad's mind. She just assumed her dad didn't care when all along he'd been grieving too and trying to take care of her in his own way. Relief flooded over Rachel as she melted into her father's embrace.

After a few minutes she pulled back as she realized it still couldn't be much after three o'clock. "Why are you home early today?"

Her dad's face lit up in remembrance. "Oh yeah! I came home early because I was so excited. Someone at work gave me two tickets to that art show you told me about." He pulled his wallet out of his pocket and opened it to reveal two beautiful orange tickets.

"Oh, Dad! Really?"

"Yes, if you'll be my date?"

"Of course!" Rachel hugged her dad again and then remembered her sketchbook. "I have something to show you too!"

Rachel raced out of the room to retrieve her sketchbook. She grabbed it off her bed and hurried back to sit with her dad. She opened the page to the songbird with the tulips.

Rachel explained her experience with the bird. She shared all the things Mrs. Keller had taught about forgiveness. She started with the rocks, then Corrie ten Boom, and ended with the weeds and tulips.

Her dad listened intently, smiling and asking questions. Rachel hadn't felt this full of love in a very long time. She leaned her head on her father's shoulder, and they looked through the rest of her sketchbook. She imagined what it might be like to go to such a special event like the art show with her dad.

She didn't need to wonder for long. The very next night, her dad wore a suit and she wore a colorful dress. They arrived at the art show and wandered in. Rachel's eyes darted around the room in hopes of catching a glimpse of Robin Heller. Rachel realized she had no idea what she looked like, though.

Mrs. Potter walked over to greet them. "Rachel! I'm so thankful you could come! I just found out your watercolor won first prize!"

Rachel looked at her dad, confused. His gaze mirrored her bewilderment. "But I didn't enter the contest, Mrs. Potter."

Mrs. Potter's eyes twinkled. "There's a teacher's choice category. Each teacher from the district can enter one painting for free. I chose yours and it won. Congratulations!" She threw her arms around Rachel in her excitement. "You are my first student ever to win first place! I knew it was a winner when you finished it. I just knew it."

Rachel beamed at her teacher's praise. Mrs. Potter led Rachel and her dad to the wall that listed the winners. They scanned the list to find Rachel's name in order to help them locate the painting.

Another art teacher pulled Mrs. Potter's attention to greet another student winner. An older gentleman in a tuxedo walked up to Rachel and her dad. He noticed where they were pointing and commented, "I really appreciate the way you blended your colors. Your piece looks like it was created by a much older artist."

Rachel blushed. "Thank you, sir."

"You are welcome. I enjoyed giving it that award," he said.

"Oh! Are you one of the judges? It's so nice to meet you. I'm Rachel. This is my dad." Rachel tried to act as grown-up as she knew how.

Her dad reached out to shake the man's hand. "I'm Christopher Landon. What's your name, sir?"

"I'm Robin Heller. It's so nice to meet you."

Rachel felt her knees weaken. "Robin Heller? *The* Robin Heller? You're not a miss... you're a . . ."

"Mister. Yes." Robin Heller grinned a welcoming smile. "I get that a lot."

Rachel felt her dad tighten his grip around her shoulders. Without his support she thought her legs wouldn't stand at all. They exchanged a few pleasantries until someone called Mr. Heller away. Once again Rachel realized things are not always as they seem.

Rachel's dad took her hand, and they followed the map to the wall that held her painting. Rachel whispered to her dad how much the prize money was. Her dad's eyebrows shot up.

Rachel's watercolor hung proudly with a blue ribbon on the upper left corner. It looked so professional with a spotlight brightening it. And there was a gold nameplate at the bottom that read,

Rachel Landon, Watercolor

Her dad looked down at her and tapped the white silk tulip on the wrist corsage he had bought her. He said, "Well done, Rachel. I'm proud of you."

The two of them stood side by side discussing her painting for a minute. Then Rachel slid her hand through her dad's arm and they explored the rest of the art show.

Together.

Discussion Questions

Teachers: For advanced discussions, projects, and more ideas to connect other subjects to this book, visit our website at
www.characterclubonline.com

1 ~ Math Madness

A)   Share about a time when you had an embarrassing moment, like Rachel's slip in the beginning of the chapter. How did you react?

B)   What subjects come easily for you in school? Which ones are difficult? How can you work with other students to fill in your weaknesses or help with theirs?

C)   Describe a time when you joined a new sport or club. How did you feel? How were you welcomed?

2 ~ The Twisted Tale

A)   Share about a time when someone said something bad about you. How did that make you feel? What are some things you did right or wrong in that situation?

B)   What do you like to do when you get home from school? If you're allowed to be home alone, what are some positive things you do with your time?

C)   In Jeanie's story, she attempted to write a limerick. Rachel knew the rules of writing limericks. Look up the rules and find what Jeanie did wrong. Try to rewrite her limerick so it's correct.

3 ~ The Sketch

A)   Rachel sketches to calm herself down. What are some things you do to calm down when you're upset?

B)   Share a story about a time you interacted with a police officer.

C)   Why do you think Rachel enjoys being with Mrs. Keller?

4 ~ The Sleepover

A)   If you could plan your own birthday party, what would it look like? Share food details, game ideas, and a schedule of activities.

B)   Share a time when someone said something untrue about you. How did you or others react? How did it make you feel?

C)   Was Rachel right to create the story with Laura? Why or why not?

5 ~ Betrayal

A)   Would you rather have Dani or Maggie for a friend? Why?

B)   How do you feel about the comments that some of the boys made to Rachel? Share a time when someone said something unkind to you.

C)   Do you think, after Jeanie saw Rachel's picture of her, that Rachel wished she'd never drawn it? Why or why not?

6 ~ Red Card

A) If you had found yourself in Rachel's position thinking you were being followed, how would you feel? What would you do differently? The same?

B) How do you think the life story of Corrie ten Boom will affect Rachel? What parts of her story inspire you?

C) Do you think if you were in Corrie's position you would help the Jews? Why or why not?

7 ~ Minefield

A) What would you write on your piece of paper about forgiveness? Whom might you need to forgive?

B) Similar to the rocks Mrs. Keller hands out, what rock are you carrying around? What can you do to let it go?

C) Sometimes mean kids get away with things. Sometimes they are caught. What do you think will happen to Dani if Valerie tells the principal what really happened?

8 ~ Botanicals

A)   Think of a smell that has special meaning to you. Share what it is and why it is special.

B)   What person or group of people around the lily pad pond do you most relate to? The teenagers, the painters, the little boys, etc.?

C)   Think of an encounter you had with an animal. What feelings did you have around the event?

9 ~ Homecoming

A)   How did Rachel change throughout the story? What are some things you think she learned?

B)   What character do you feel had the most impact on Rachel? How? Why?

C)   What have you learned about forgiveness from Rachel's story? How might this make an impact on your future decisions?

Glossary

Amygdala *noun* - a ganglion of the limbic system adjoining the temporal lobe of the brain and involved in emotions of fear and aggression.

Boutonniere *noun* - a flower or small bouquet worn, usually by a man, in the buttonhole of a lapel.

Cairn *noun* - a heap of stones set up as a landmark, monument, tombstone, etc.

Cellophane *noun* - a transparent, paperlike product used to wrap and package food, etc.

Chide(d) *verb* - to express disapproval of; scold; reproach

Concentration Camp *noun* - a guarded compound for the detention or imprisonment of aliens, members of ethnic minorities, political opponents, etc., especially any of the camps established by the Nazis prior to and during World War II for the confinement and persecution of prisoners.

Corridor *noun* - a gallery or passage connecting parts of a building; hallway.

Fitfully *adjective* - coming, appearing, acting, etc., in fits or by spells; recurring irregularly.

Mortified (mortify) *verb* - to humiliate or shame, as by injury to one's pride or self-respect.

Nemeses *plural noun* - something that a person cannot conquer, achieve, etc.

Occupant(s) *noun* - a person, family, group, or organization that lives in, occupies, or has quarters or space in or on something.

Perpetrator *noun* - a person who commits, an illegal, criminal, or evil act.

Perseverating *verb* - to repeat something insistently or redundantly.

Prefrontal Cortex *noun* - of, relating to, or located near the forward part of a frontal lobe or structure of the brain or head. The outer layer of an organ or other body part such as the kidney or the adrenal gland.

Ration *noun* - a fixed allowance of provisions or food, especially for soldiers or sailors or for civilians during a shortage.

Regime *noun* - a government in power.

Restorative Justice *noun* - a theory and method in criminal justice in which it is arranged that the victim and the community receive restitution from the offender.

Reverie *noun* - a daydream.

Solitary Confinement *noun* - to shut or keep a prisoner in a cell in which he or she is completely isolated from others.

Variegated *adjective* - exhibiting different colors, especially as irregular patches or streaks.

Xeriscape *noun* - environmental design of residential and park land using various methods for minimizing the need for water use.

About Robin Heller

Robin Heller, a character in this book, *really* is an artist who *really* drew a comic strip named Mukluk & Honisukle in the mid-1990s. He also *really* did a school program called LET's DRAW. Rachel fictionally mistook him for a woman, but he *really* often found people waiting for a woman to show up if they'd never met him before. The comic Jeanie referred to is included below.

Robin Heller also illustrated *Benjamin Blair and the Case of the Missing Noun Hound,* the first book in the Character Club Lil Sibs series (see next page). You can learn more about the *real* Robin Heller in *Mukluk & Honisukle: 50th Anniversary Edition,* which includes over two thousand comic strips. It is available on Amazon.

Oh, and Robin Heller is *really* Allie Slocum's dad.

Reprinted with permission

Other Books By Allie Slocum

Jeanie Blair's younger triplet brothers get a journey of their own in the clever mystery *Benjamin Blair and the Case of the Missing Noun Hound*. Ben's teacher is missing her favorite puppet so she can't teach about nouns...or can she?

Want to read more about Jeanie, Ethan, and all the other Character Club kids? Then join Jeanie in the first book in the Character Club series as she struggles toward compassion while trying to become a famous author.

Character Club Series

Jeanie Blair
Author
Extraordinaire
A Journey Toward Compassion

Once upon a time...

by Allie Slocum

And then join Ethan in the second book in the
Character Club series as he struggles toward
integrity while trying to overcome his fear of
heights and impress his friends.

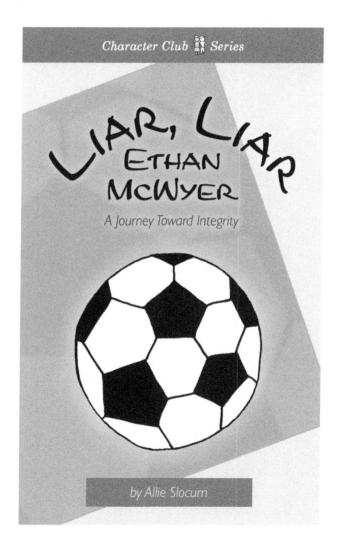

Character Club 👫 Series

LIAR, LIAR
ETHAN
McWYER

A Journey Toward Integrity

by Allie Slocum

Made in the USA
Columbia, SC
17 May 2022

60541450R00108